EDITORS
Susan Burmeister-Brown   Linda B. Swanson-Davies

CONSULTING EDITORS
Kimberly Bennett   Allyson Bourke
J. Jackson Reynolds   Roz Wais
Chanda Wakefield

COPY EDITOR
Scott Stuart Allie

PROOFREADER
Rachel Penn

TYPESETTING & LAYOUT
Paul Morris

ADMINISTRATIVE ASSISTANT
Kaylin Elaine Dodge

COVER ARTIST
Jane Zwinger

STORY ILLUSTRATOR
Jon Leon

PUBLISHED QUARTERLY
in spring, summer, fall, and winter by **Glimmer Train Press, Inc.**
710 SW Madison Street, Suite 504, Portland, Oregon 97205-2900
Telephone: 503/221-0836   Facsimile: 503/221-0837
www.glimmertrain.com
PRINTED IN U.S.A.
Indexed in *The American Humanities Index.*

Glimmer Train (ISSN #1055-7520), registered in U.S. Patent and Trademark Office, is published quarterly, $32 per year in the U.S., by Glimmer Train Press, Inc., Suite 504, 710 SW Madison, Portland, OR 97205. Periodicals postage paid at Portland, OR, and additional mailing offices. POSTMASTER: Send address changes to Glimmer Train Press, Inc., Suite 504, 710 SW Madison, Portland, OR 97205.

ISSN # 1055-7520, **ISBN # 1-880966-38-7**, CPDA BIPAD # 79021

DISTRIBUTION: Bookstores can purchase *Glimmer Train Stories* through these distributors:
Ingram Periodicals, 1226 Heil Quaker Blvd., LaVergne, TN 37086
IPD, 674 Via de la Valle, #204, Solana Beach, CA 92075
Peribo PTY Ltd., 58 Beaumont Rd., Mt. Kuring-Gai, NSW 2080, AUSTRALIA
Ubiquity, 607 Degraw St., Brooklyn, NY 11217

SUBSCRIPTION SVCS: EBSCO, Faxon, Readmore, Turner Subscriptions, Blackwell's UK

Subscription rates: One year, $32 within the U.S. (Visa/MC/check).
Airmail to Canada, $43; outside North America, $54.
Payable by Visa/MC or check for U.S. dollars drawn on a U.S. bank.

Dedication

We dedicate this issue to our dad, Henry J. Burmeister. At 83, even with congestive heart failure, he is still entertaining and educating and energizing the rest of us.

As he was being wheeled into surgery recently, *he* was trying to soothe *us* by joking, making us all laugh, and he said, "I'm going to have to pass the hat. And I don't want to hear the clink of coins—I'm listening for the rustle of paper!" And then a moment later, with a wink and a touch, he added, "Put *that* in your magazine."

He told us afterwards, "thankful to be here," that his one regret was that he hadn't written a book. "A lot of interesting things have happened to me. Mixed with a little humor, I think it could have been something."

Linda & Susan

It's wrong to believe that only professional writers can write things of value. So, I'm trying to convince these groups that all the intentions they've had for writing are worthy; and I am there to give them permission to write—as if they needed it, though often they do—and to convince them that writing leaves a trace, and there wouldn't be a trace of what they thought or felt or knew about their families, or what they believe about God, about the kinds of stories they want to tell. There will be no trace of that unless they write it.

—Charles Baxter,
interviewed by Stewart David Ikeda

CONTENTS

CONTENTS

Gerard Varni

No, I don't have a clubfoot, but my
father, Laius, is taking the picture.

Gerard Varni lives with his wife, Mary Ann, and two children, Emily and
Brooks, in Manhattan Beach, California. He works when he must and
writes when he can, although often it's the other way around. He graduated from Loyola Marymount University with degrees in philosophy and
English; he earned an MA in English from the same school. This is the first
time his work has appeared, as he puts it, "in one of the big guns."

GERARD VARNI
Death's Noisy Herald

FIRST-PLACE WINNER
Short-Story Award
for New Writers

*T*he bastards will howl. That much Baxter Bright
knows. At the moment, though, he's more concerned with
getting there. Driving is difficult. His arm movement is lim-
ited; turning his head to look for other cars is simply impossible. That's because he's wrapped from waist to neck in foam
rubber.

He'd gone to a sporting-goods store and bought one of
those mats you put under a sleeping bag. Eight feet long, two
inches thick. It wraps around him twice. Of course, he had to
cut arm holes, and it took about a half roll of duct tape to
secure the thing.

He fully expects to be taunted. And why not? He resembles
nothing so much as a human hot dog, a walking, talking
Hebrew National. But he's desperate, and he consoles himself
with the old saw that desperate men do desperate things.
Something like that. He isn't about to miss the game. Poker,

Glimmer Train Stories, Issue 39, Summer 2001
©*2001 Gerard Varni*

once a week, for a couple of years now. Fairly high stakes. Thousand-dollar buy in, five-dollar minimum bet. On a good night, the winner walks with five grand.

Last week, he wore a musty, old ski sweater and a down jacket, until he couldn't stand it anymore because of the heat, which gave him a rash. And even with all that gear on, everyone could still hear the thing. His heart, that is. Actually, it's a valve, a mechanical heart valve. And when it really gets going, it emits a moaning, whistling sound, like wind rushing through trees.

Three months ago, when he'd had the surgery, nobody had warned him about the noise. He woke up in the hospital room the day after the operation, nobody around, and heard an odd sound. *Drip, drip, drip*, like a leaky pipe. He actually got out of the damn bed and looked around for it. He was hooked up to a heart monitor, and he imagined the thing shorting out from the flood. When he couldn't find anything, he lay back down on the bed, out of breath. And the noise was even louder. Then it came to him. The only plumbing problem was inside his chest.

When he's relaxed, it sounds something like *thrum swish click, thrum swish click, thrum swish click*. As his pulse quickens, though, the volume and the pitch increase, becoming an annoying trill, which ultimately yields to a loud, sibilant cry. He's about six-foot-four, pretty good sized, not fat or anything, just big. The doctor told him the valve they had to use was a little larger than normal.

"That's why it's exceptionally loud," he said.

"You're goddamned right," Baxter said. "I can take my pulse without touching my body."

The doctor laughed. "Listen, think of it this way," he reasoned, "as long as you hear it, you're not dead."

So there he is a month later at the poker game, and he'd already told the guys about looking for leaks in the hospital and waking up groggy some nights, rolling out of bed to shut the window because it sounded like it was raining. Anyway, they know the thing makes noise. And they know it irks him, so they don't give him too much shit. When the heart is beating at its normal rhythm—72 bpm—it's hard for other people to hear the *click*, unless they're really paying attention. The thing is, though, when the son of a bitch winds up, the whirring comes loud and fast and sometimes it sounds like a hundred tiny sleigh bells. Clearly audible over normal conversation. So the first time he finds himself staring at a good hand, he gets excited, which, of course, agitates the valve. But he can't help it. There's five hundred stinking dollars in the pot.

Then, across the table, Tom frowns, cocks his head, and says, "What the fuck is that noise?"

"It's Bax," says Pete. "Sounds like it's coming out of his ears." Suddenly, they all get it, stare down at their cards, and the room becomes even quieter.

"Whose bet?" Baxter stammers, looking at a natural boat, kings full of deuces.

"Yours," says Pete.

A hundred, he says, tossing it into the pot. The heart sounds like some sort of industrial turbine. The guys glance at each other, but they all call the bet. He lays down the boat, enough to beat Tom's flush, and pulls the pot toward him. It was the last decent pot he won that night. From then on, every time they heard the valve begin to tootle, they threw in their cards. Of course, nobody said anything, but then nobody had to. They may as well have dealt his cards face up. He was pinched.

The worst time is when he's lying on his side in bed. With one ear buried in the pillow, the noise is almost intolerable, something akin to a leaf-blower yowling outside the window. Lying there, with this terrible screech emanating from his chest, blaring from his open mouth, he thinks about jet planes and jack hammers and nuclear explosions. He doesn't have quiet thoughts.

There are more tranquil alternatives. Organic valves, for instance, which are harvested from pigs and cows, are far quieter. A porcine valve (as well as its bovine equivalent) is effectively silent. After all, it's real tissue. Problem is, they only last eight or nine years. So a relatively young valve recipient might require three or more replacement surgeries—com-

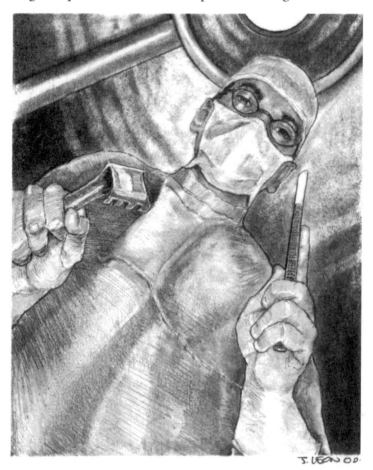

J. LEON OD.

plete with bone saws and rib spreaders and chest-slicing scalpels. After his cardiologist had presented Baxter with these facts (the bit about bone saws and rib spreaders was particularly convincing), he agreed to the artificial valve.

When he was a child, eight or nine, Baxter contracted rheumatic fever. It didn't seem so bad at the time. Hell, it got him out of Sister Mary Joseph's third-grade gulag for a month. But, apparently, it was the genesis of his current condition. The virus produces calcium deposits, which accumulate and harden in heart valves, causing the muscle to pump blood less efficiently. Eventually, the put-upon organ begins to sputter, causing weakness, fainting, and other unsettling symptoms— like the feeling of imminent death.

Baxter experienced all of these one day while walking toward his car in the gym parking lot after his usual workout. First, he had trouble catching his breath. Then, he was suffused with an eerie warmth, followed by intense dizziness, as he fell to his knees and his vision sped away down a dark tunnel. The next thing he recalls is staring up at a heaving cleavage. An amply endowed young woman in a tight outfit was bent over him, slapping his cheek and breathlessly intoning, "Are you all right? Sir? Are you all right?"

Two weeks later—after a flurry of EKGs and sonograms, thallium stress tests and twenty-four-hour Holter monitors— he was wandering around his hospital room like a hallucinogenic plumber looking for leaks.

He pulls the car over to the curb in front of Tom's place, a smallish, well-kept house with a surfeit of overgrown bushes encroaching on windows that are all covered with wrought-iron bars. He yanks the key from the ignition, inhales and exhales deeply. He has a wad of money in the front pocket of his Levi's. He's prepared for their ridicule. He knows the valve is well into its gruesome little symphony, because he feels his heart dancing in his chest. With the thick foam wrap, however, it is at least a subdued composition.

Next, his knuckles rap the door. He breathes heavily, waits. Tom answers, looks him up and down with a slightly raised eyebrow.

"Well, Bax, thought you'd skipped out on us."

Baxter makes his way through the front door, awkwardly, swinging from side to side the way a refrigerator does when it's moved. He sees the rest of the guys sitting at the table, counting chips, drinking beer. They look up, see him, glance over at Tom who's still holding the door open. Nobody says anything at first, there's just silence, but he senses a collective "What the fuck?" hanging in the air. Then Pete, who is apparently in mid-chug when Baxter walks in, can't control himself any longer and erupts with a deep gagging sound, which precipitates a gusher of beer from his mouth and nostrils. He's choking and stuff is still dripping out of his face when the rest of the crowd loses it. Since they seem to be at least as amused by Pete's nose geyser as they are by the six-foot-four-inch foam-wrapped goon in the doorway, Baxter laughs a bit, too.

There aren't many questions at first. After all, everyone knows why he's resorted to such disturbing measures. So the cards start to slide.

"Jacks or better, trips to win." Pete deals, after having mopped up his yeasty face.

Baxter sits ruler-straight in his chair, primarily because that's the only option. He pulls his cards toward him and watches sadly as one slips from his grasp and flutters to the floor. He looks down at it, a deuce; of course it's landed face up. He leans to the left, makes a vain attempt to bend over and snag the damn thing. But his arm doesn't move past forty-five degrees in relation to the side of his body. So when he leans down, he overshoots the card by a foot. It's an awkward moment, but the others want to let him do this himself. They don't even look down, don't want to see the card.

Finally, after a humiliating minute of bouncing and grunting and failing to even touch the wayward card, he gives up and says, "Okay, everyone, it's a deuce of clubs and I can't fucking reach it because I'm wearing a fucking hot-dog costume so you bastards won't hear my fucking valve when I get a good hand and get all excited. There, it's all out in the fucking open. Now, Tom, would you please be kind enough to fetch my fucking deuce of clubs for me? Thank you."

As the evening wears on, his sense of indignity increases. Dealing is out of the question, of course, and he experiences the same temperature discomfort that he'd encountered with the sweater and down jacket. Worse still, after the first dozen hands or so, he hasn't been dealt anything decent anyway. The valve purrs quietly along, *thrum swish click.*

At one point, he glimpses his reflection in a window. From this angle, he doesn't see a hot dog so much as an overgrown hors d'oeuvre, his head a cocktail olive perched atop something doughy. Suddenly, he is struck by the utter absurdity of the situation. And it's no longer comical; he is overcome with a vivid sensation of dread. He feels a bead of perspiration slide down his chest, thinks of his heart and the thin veil that separates life and death. The valve seems ambiguous. Miraculous, certainly, but foreign, a pathogen boring away inside his chest. Shaken, he gets up between hands and walks out. Waddles, actually. Doesn't say a word, not thanks, not fuck you all for having healthy hearts, nothing. Just shimmies through the door and closes it quietly behind him.

He drives home, walks immediately to the kitchen, takes out a knife, and begins tearing through the tape and foam rubber, trailing the shredded remnants of his masquerade into the bedroom. He falls into bed exhausted, angry, hopeless.

Eventually, he falls asleep to the metronomic rhythms of the valve. He dreams.

It is the moment of his death. He is weak, confused; he concentrates on gathering his breath and all his senses. With each inhalation particles of light descend into his heart, illuminating a path he must take. He can no longer see, nor taste, nor speak. He is becoming something entirely other, withdrawing into the heart. He cannot think, nor touch. Beyond knowing, he encounters the heart, which has become merely a point of light, and by that light he departs through the apertures of his body. All the vital breaths, and thus his life, depart with him, opening up into the air and outward, forming a hole like the center of a wheel. He passes through this opening, moving up toward the sun. All that exists unfolds before him and the sun, too, opens up a luminous hole through which he passes, still and still moving, up toward the moon, toward an existence free from grief, beyond the world of fear and desire. And in the morning, his eyes tick open in perfect cadence with the snapping of the valve.

It is made from a hard, polished, black material called pyrolitic carbon. The valve. It is round, with two half-moon-shaped leaflets forming its center. These leaflets, also made of pyrolitic carbon, pivot shut with each heartbeat to close the orifice and control blood flow. On the outside of the ring-like valve, there is a sewing cuff made of Teflon and Dacron, through which the surgeon runs the thread that connects the device to human tissue.

He knows all this because he's seen a valve, studied it. Before the surgery, his cardiologist gave him one to take home. He lived with it for a couple days, opening and closing the leaflets, holding it up to the light and peering through the Dacron cuff. He held it under the faucet in the kitchen, moved it in and out of the stream, observed as the water worked the leaflets. He imagined it inside his chest, opening and closing a thousand times each day. But the noise, that he didn't contemplate.

In the following days, he finds himself being swept aimlessly from one disparate moment to the next, seeking external distractions—movies, food, booze, work. He's a technical writer for a software company, monotonous work, twisting the tortured language of engineers into the dull prose of user's manuals. But now he throws himself into it with a sense of mission and renewed vigor. It's a way of suppressing valve thoughts for eight solid hours at a stretch. He doesn't work in silence, though, as he once had. It's no longer an ally. Yes, he still cocoons himself inside a windowless office, where the air is still and warm, almost stifling. But now he has a compact-disc player and earphones, and he does his writing while listening to Blind Boy Fuller and Segovia and Mozart's *Requiem* at considerable volume.

After work, he goes to a bar and throws down a few beers, plays a little pool, flirts with the women, knowing full well he can never take them home to his soundless apartment. He'd made that mistake once. She was a regular, small and sleek, with wild red hair and a sensuous South Carolina drawl. The guys at the bar called her Wing-nut; they had fantasies of planting her atop their prone bodies and giving her a good spin.

One night, she comes home with Baxter and she isn't shy about why. As soon as they get through the door, she is tugging at his clothes while her tongue flicks away at his ear. They stumble into the bedroom, fall onto the bed, and kiss urgently, roughly. And then she is naked, on top of him, grasping behind for his cock. His heart throbs warm and hard in his chest, and the valve wails like a warning siren. She, breathless and still searching, says, "Do you hear that noise? What is it?" And he has to tell her that it's him. She's nice about it, actually. She giggles and says, "How cool." Then she puts her head to his chest and begins humming at the same pitch. But it's over for him; he shrinks faster than a hot popsicle. He thanks her for understanding, says that she's wonderful, really, but that he's tired. When he shuts the door after her, he leans his head against it and kicks the jamb as hard as he can, again and again, until the blood shows through his socks.

He starts going to concerts, seeks out bands he's never heard of purely for their sonic prowess. Groups like Sexy Death Soda, The Faggot Punks, and Dog Party, who play long, searing sets. And afterwards, he walks out with the discordant notes ricocheting inside his head like frenzied atoms. The roar lasts for hours, inundating his senses until long after he goes to bed and begins the dream of dying.

This new lifestyle, though, this immersion in tumult and din, begins to diminish him both physically and mentally. He is chronically exhausted. And there are times when he is anxious almost to the point of panic. He goes to the doctor, who prescribes Xanax for the anxiety, saying it will also help him sleep. Soon, he's eating Xanax like candy corn. Still, he sleeps fitfully and often wakes in the morning disoriented and slick with sweat. He drinks more, eats less. And then one day at work, he feels his heart skip a beat. He tears the headphones off and waits. It happens again. He can feel it in his throat, the disrupted rhythm, and he is quickly enveloped by a sickening sense of warmth and dread. When it flutters again, he panics and the valve clicks even faster. And louder.

He begins to doubt his sanity, visits a psychiatrist, who teaches him to meditate, to concentrate on his breathing until he is calm. Insisting that breath is the bridge to consciousness, the psychiatrist tells him, "Now, as you slowly inhale, say to yourself, 'I am breathing in a long breath, and thus I teach myself to breathe in.' And as you exhale, again slowly, think, 'I am breathing out a long breath, and thus I teach myself to breathe out.' "

The breathing technique is an ancient Buddhist sutra. The psychiatrist calls it *mindfulness*, says it is a miracle by which human beings can master and restore themselves.

"Whenever a crisis arises, you must resolve to maintain self control and keep a calm heart. And you can do this through mindfulness, by living in the moment of each breath."

Baxter overcomes a cynical urge to label this advice mystical bullshit. He is desperate. So he tries it, practices meditating, taking long, purposeful breaths, and following the rhythms of his pulse until he is pervaded by a sensation of peace. He does this for a month and, to his utter amazement, discovers that it helps. Soon, he is able to work without headphones; he cuts back on the booze, sleeps better. He even summons the courage to rejoin the poker game. Which is where it all falls apart again.

The details are insignificant, yet entirely axiomatic. The struggle begins with his first good hand, two pair—bullets over kings. Despite his resolute meditative efforts, Baxter's valve noise suddenly ratchets from a barely audible *thrum swish click* to an eye-averting roar. Only this time the biological concerto is augmented by the sound of his ludicrous heavy breathing. He loses his concentration, and instead of simply breathing in and out slowly, he begins sucking and blowing with a disturbing fervor. Soon, he is lightheaded and dark spots whirl counterclockwise through his field of vision; the sensation of looming unconsciousness washes over him like a soporific. He drops his cards, still gasping and heaving, propelling himself into hypoxia. Pete yells for someone to call 911.

Then, Baxter is vaguely aware of chairs being pushed back wildly and tumbling over, beer bottles crashing, an infinity of strange noises sweeping him toward darkness. Oddly, though, in his barely conscious state, flailing like a lunatic unhinged, he is suffused with a violent thirst for life.

The next day, after an embarrassing junket to the emergency room, he's back at his cardiologist's office. All the tests are normal, the doctor tells him, nothing wrong with the heart or the valve.

"It was a panic attack," he says. "Classic symptoms. You get yourself all worked up, adrenaline kicks in, your body's fight-or-flight mechanism goes into overdrive. It's a primal response to overwhelming fear. Now you know what *Homo erectus* felt like when a saber-tooth tiger wandered into the cave."

Is he taking the anticoagulant? Yes, Baxter tells him. That's good. Drinking alcohol? Again, yes. "Not good," he snorts. "The combination of the alcohol and the anticoagulant could very well precipitate this sort of an attack." In fact, the doctor tells Baxter, he's sure of it.

"How are you sleeping?" he asks, scribbling something onto his chart.

He ignores the question. "Listen, doctor, I want to do it over. What I mean is … I mean the valve, the noise, I can't live with it. It's gonna kill me. I want an organic valve, the cow or the pig. Anything that doesn't make the goddamn noise."

The doctor stops writing, looks up as if Baxter had just told him he wanted a sex change. His glasses slip from the bridge of his nose, and he grabs wildly to snare them. The chart falls to the ground. "You're kidding, right?" he chuckles. Baxter shakes his head, looks away. "You're not kidding. Are you fucking crazy"?

"Pretty damn close, if you want to know the truth."

"It's out of the question," he stammers. "You don't need it. The valve you have now is working perfectly. Consider yourself lucky. A lot of poor slobs don't make it *this* far."

Then Baxter is up off the chair, in the doctor's face, close enough to smell his sterile breath. He starts pleading, frantic: "Before the surgery, you said an organic valve was an alternative. You told me it wouldn't last as long, but you didn't say it would be quieter. You didn't tell me about the noise *this* would make." He stabs at his chest with an index finger.

"Mr. Bright... Baxter, there is no valid medical reason to replace that valve. I'm sorry. You're talking about elective surgery. We don't *do* elective heart surgery. Insurance companies don't *pay* for elective heart surgery. Organic valves aren't available for *elective heart surgery!*" The doctor hammers these last three words in staccato fashion, his voice rising, his face florid and moist.

"What do you mean the valves aren't available? Why not?"

"You're not hearing me, Baxter. The point is you don't need it. You'll become accustomed to the sound of the valve, trust me." He puts his hand on Baxter's shoulder. "In the meantime, we can up the Xanax a bit, go to two milligrams. That'll take care of the anxiety. You'll sleep better. And by the way, cut out the booze."

He tears the hastily written prescription from the pad, gives it to Baxter, shakes his hand vigorously. There is something cryptic and unsettling about the way the doctor looks at him. Fear? Exasperation? Baxter isn't sure.

"You're going to be fine," he says in an overly indulgent tone. "I want to see you again in a month. Any problems before then, don't hesitate to call."

Baxter walks out into the bright sunlight, sneezes reflexively, and thinks he feels his heart jump and flutter. He drives to work and requests a leave of absence. Not citing any specific reason, he simply fills out the paperwork, gathers his few things—including his discs and CD player, some reference books and a container of mint tea—and leaves without waiting to hear from his supervisor. It doesn't matter. In his mind, he's begun separating reality into compartments, calculating the value of each small room in accordance with its proximity to his own distress.

Just after the surgery, he truly looked forward to living, welcomed the reprieve he'd been given with grateful anticipation. Now, however, he views the machine in his chest as little more than death's noisy herald. Extraordinary, yes, it will open and close forty million times in a year—forty million times! Yet each cycle is an audible alert, an intimation of mortality. The Dacron, the carbon, the pyrolite, all gleaming reminders that, really, he's been cheated. Whereas once he genuinely cared about the suffering and joy of others, that is all secondary now to the question of his own existence. Living and dying are now two faces of the same reality. And he feels as though he's lost the courage to endure either. He hardly knows how to live anymore, yet he is equally bewildered by the problem of how to die.

And perhaps that's it, *the problem of dying.* Maybe it isn't a problem at all. Conceivably, it's just something he has to experience more intimately. He remembers the psychiatrist asking in one of their sessions if he was afraid of death. "I'm not sure," he'd replied, "but I suppose so."

"That's not healthy, Baxter. If one doesn't know how to die, one can hardly know how to live."

That night the dream is different. This time he is floating inside a sort of medieval stone tower. At the bottom of this dark, dank structure, there is a naked corpse. He tries to look away, but he's transfixed. The body is decomposing. It swells, distends, turns colors—first a greenish-grey, then a curious violet. It is being eaten away by worms, until only bits of flesh cling to the bones. Soon, only the white bones remain, which in turn are slowly worn away into dust. Then, he is aware of a noise, an eerie scraping. He looks up to see the roof of the tower sliding away, admitting a shaft of sunlight that illuminates the pile of dust. It rises inside the brilliant conduit of light, ascending to the level where he is floating and continuing upward. He watches it rise toward a blue circle of sky outside the tower. But the moment it clears the top of the shelter, there is a tremendous blast of wind. And the heap of dust is carried off to a place he cannot see.

The next day he spends a lot of time walking and thinking, planning. It's hot, and there's little wind. He's not familiar with the noises of the city on a weekday, but he welcomes the cacophony: the grinding gears of delivery trucks, the blaring taxi horns, and the omnipresent *beep beep beep* of garbage trucks in reverse. This comforting white noise washes over his senses, its narcotic effect enabling him to concentrate on the blueprint he's forming in his mind. He stops at a sporting-goods store, then moves on to a military-surplus outlet, and finally a liquor store.

He glances at his watch, sees that it's almost 4:00 P.M., smiles. He's gone almost the whole day without hearing the valve. He imagines what this would be like every day. Back at his apartment, he clicks on the stereo, throws open the windows, and begins unpacking his purchases. From the sporting-goods store, a knife and a box of ammunition; from the military-surplus outlet, a musty, old army-issue backpack; and from the liquor store, a bag of ice and bottle of vodka. The ice and vodka he puts in the freezer. The knife and the ammunition he drops in the backpack's front compartment. Then he walks to his closet, reaches up, and pulls down a handgun, a Ruger GP 100 .357 magnum. He'd won it in a poker game years ago, but had never fired it; he'd kept it around, without bullets, just in case he'd had to scare an intruder. He puts the gun in the front of the backpack with the knife and the ammo. Then he lays down for a nap. No dreams, he tells himself. He understands already.

His eyes flicker open at 10:20. The apartment is dark, save for the weak red glow of the numbers on the alarm clock. The stereo is still playing and, in fact, seems louder, perhaps because the noise on the street has subsided. He rises groggily, slams the windows shut, punches the stereo off, then sits back down on his bed to listen. It's there, in its tamer disposition. *Thrum swish click. Thrum swish click.* He reaches for the Xanax on the nightstand, grabs two, then walks to the kitchen and takes the vodka and the bag of ice out of the freezer. He cracks open the vodka, washes down the pills, then drops the bag of ice on the floor to loosen it up. He pours the ice into the main compartment of the backpack, takes another long pull on the vodka, then shoves the bottle into the ice and zips up the backpack.

One can hardly live if one doesn't know how to die, he thinks as he walks to his car. The canvas pack is cool against his back, exaggerating the sensation of the warm, still air. He slings the pack onto the front seat of his old brown Celica—hatchback, automatic, with rear-window louvers and a spoiler. It's always been reliable. Traffic is light, and he eases onto the freeway, settles in to the far right lane, turns on the radio, and reaches for the vodka. He's driving east, away from the city, away from the beggars, the bosses, the doctors, the insurance bastards, the whole cluster of chaos and humiliation. It will be quiet where he is going. He reaches over and nudges the radio volume up a bit.

After two hours and one hundred miles, he pulls off the freeway onto a two-lane highway that will wind through flat, scrubby farmland up into the foothills, then twist across a squat range of mountains and, eventually, descend into a state-long stretch of desert. He isn't going as far as the road will take him, though. When he smells cows, he pulls to the side of the road, into the dirt, near an old stand of eucalyptus trees. He cuts the lights and reaches for the backpack, which drips ice water as he pulls it over his shoulder. He takes the vodka bottle out; it's still half full, but he throws it to the ground after one last gulp. He pours the water out of the backpack, looks inside, and sees there is still ice left. He unzips his pants, begins to pee, swaying side to side as he does. He's drunk, but he tells himself that at least he knows he's drunk. "Can't hardly live 'til you know how to die." He says it out loud this time, belches, then zips up and trudges toward the trees.

No sense in going too far, he reasons. Not now, anyway. So he stops, kneels down, sets the dripping pack beside him. Suddenly, he is thinking about the two dreams—his death dreams—the luminous rising, the rotting body, the dust. And it occurs to him that there is some mystical, ineluctable quality to dreams, that all *this* is inescapable, has been since the day the birth slime oozed from his lungs.

He reaches into the backpack and pulls out the gun. In the faint light of the half-moon, he sees a glint catch the silver barrel. He points it toward the field, pulls the trigger once, twice. *Click, click.* That sound. So familiar. He listens to his heart, to the valve. The night is hot and windless, and quiet. *Thrum swish click.* He listens, looks up, whispers it to the trees. *Thrum swish click.* He reaches into the backpack and takes a round from the box of ammunition. Then he pushes the cylinder release on the gun, holds it up and looks at the moon through the five holes. He spins the cylinder, and the moon seems to flutter like an old moving picture. *Thrum swish click.* He blows through the cylinder, spins it clockwise, then the other way. He closes his eyes, places the bullet into one of the chambers, then spins it again once, twice. *Thrum swish click.* He turns the gun toward him, *thrum swish click*, points it at his chest, pulls it away. *Thrum swish click.* Presses it against his temple, again pulls it away, then places the barrel in his mouth. *Thrum swish click.* He waits for a moment when he is thinking of absolutely nothing in this world but dying. Then he pulls the trigger. *Click*. Fine, he thinks, dropping the gun into the dirt. That's decided. Now for the living part. It is an urge so irresistible that it has the force of doom.

Emerging from the line of trees, he encounters a low fence and, on its opposite side, a field of tall sunflowers. Beyond the sunflowers, in the listless moonlight, he is barely able to make out a group of white buildings. He jumps the fence, pushes his way through the maze of sunflowers, and walks toward the buildings, which resemble soup cans sliced in half lengthwise and shoved into the dirt.

As he crisscrosses shallow drainage ditches, he is aware that the stink of the place is intensifying. Doubtless, the ditches are conduits for animal waste, fertilizers, and pesticides, but the thought doesn't deter him. About twenty yards from the buildings now, he sinks to one knee and notices for the first time that his heart is agitated, the metallic sound of the valve is different, and much louder. It is snapping and whirring, emitting a high-pitched tone like the mewling of a cat. The stench is overwhelming, and he understands now that the source is a sort of pond or lagoon in front of the buildings. It must be the animals' collected waste—pure shit and piss and blood—a foul miasma deepened by the odor of nitrogen and sulfur and ammonia.

He walks toward the three white metal structures. Each has a sign appended to it: *Breeding Room, Growing Room, Finishing Room*. He walks into the building marked *Growing Room*, careful to shut the door quietly behind him. Then he pauses, lets his eyes adjust to the room's dim light, which comes from a single bulb hanging at the far end. He is almost overcome by the fetid reek of... hogs? He'd expected cows, but this, the pigs, this is fine, even better, he tells himself. He puts the pack down carefully, leans it against a wall opposite the nearest enclosure. There's still a bit of ice left and some cold water. I'll find someone else, he thinks. Another doctor. And no need for mechanical parts.

He takes the knife out, unsheathes it. A snuffling, rooting noise permeates the room; it's loud, but he doesn't hear it, not over the valve's snap and whir. He steps to the enclosure, looks in at the pig, which is massive, five hundred pounds at least, much larger than he'd thought a pig could grow. It doesn't seem to mind his presence, even as he mounts the steel bars of the fence.

He leaps down on top of the hog, punches the knife into its thick, stubbled flesh as hard as he can. The animal erupts not with a squeal but with a deep, screeching howl, whipping its head around. It twists and thrashes, throws him off. He lands hard, slipping on the animal's piss and shit as he tries to get up. The pig skitters and lurches toward him, knife still protruding from its back. He lunges, gets both hands on the knife, tears it free as the pig slams him against the railing. He scrambles up several rungs, feels the enraged animal gnashing at his legs.

He sees blood spilling from the wound in the pig's back, hears the shrieking and yowling of the other animals in the room. Then he raises the knife above his head with both hands, frantic, breathing in staccato bursts. His heart is throbbing, and the whir of the valve roars in his head. He slams the knife into the pig's back, hits bone, feels his fingers slip past the handguard and slide down the shaft of the knife. The pig stops thrashing but continues to grunt and wail.

Baxter squats next to it, breathless, wipes his face instinctively, smearing it with an admixture of blood and filth. He feels as though he's climbed a great height, abolished every contrast between the world and himself. He looks at his tremulous, bleeding hands, then into the vacant eyes of the soughing pig. He feels sorry for the animal and coughs to quell a faint tickling of remorse. Still, he reasons, the two have arrived at an inescapable juncture.

"Fucking beast," he whispers, "don't you know how to die?"

SHORT-STORY AWARD FOR NEW WRITERS
1st-, 2nd-, and 3rd-Place Winners

First-place winner: GERARD VARNI

Gerard Varni receives $1200 for his first-place story, "Death's Noisy Herald," which begins on page 7, preceded by his profile on page 6.

Second-place winner: C. V. DAVIS

C. V. Davis receives $500 for "Begin with Where They Are." He is a PhD student in creative writing at Florida State University, where he has been a Kingsbury Fellow in Fiction and now serves as fiction editor for Sundog: The Southeast Review. Davis lives in Tallahassee with his wife and daughter.

C V Davis

"Begin with Where They Are"

I wait by the gate, a swell of uncertainty flitting around inside me like butterflies fighting a battle royal. My hands are empty, lonely even, though they at least find one another in a clench behind my waist.

Third-place winner: ALAN McWHIRTER

Alan McWhirter receives $300 for "The Fire God." Born in 1961 in Glasgow, Scotland, Alan McWhirter lives with his wife and three children in Uppsala, Sweden. A microbiologist by trade, he now works as a scientific writer and reads his short stories to anyone who will listen. He builds stone ovens and cooks in his spare time.

"The Fire God"

But he'd give anything to hear her say, The oven'll sure look pretty when it's done. He wants to be lying beside a lover whom he can shake awake now and take to the window, stand behind her with his arms over her breasts and kiss her neck and show her what he's done.

We invite you to our website (www.glimmertrain.com) to see a listing of the top twenty-five winners and finalists, and online submission procedures. We thank all entrants for sending in their work.

Tiffany Drever

This is the first photograph ever taken of me—
I'm just a few hours old. Occasionally, in moments
of anxiety, I believe I still assume this posture.

Tiffany Drever was raised in San Francisco, and now lives in New York City, where she teaches humanities at the Cooper Union. She recently received her PhD in English literature from the University of California at Irvine, as well as an MFA from the same university. This is her first published fiction.

Tiffany E. Drever

TIFFANY DREVER
Lesser Waterways

*J*he affair began, as affairs often do, because each dreamed of the other, first at night, and then more and more often during the day.

Emily had the first dream. In it, Chase was giving a convocation to the boarding school where he was headmaster. Students were beginning to assemble on a wide grassy lawn on a hazy, uncomfortable spring morning when he grabbed her by the hand. He took her behind the damp stone chapel and kissed her, then ran his tongue down her neck and under her collarbones. She woke up gasping.

He dreamed he was on a sailboat with her and it was about to storm. She pulled him below deck onto a pile of ropes and tangled their limbs in them. He woke up frantic with their rocking, unable to look at his wife.

After that it was natural that they should pause in the courses of their days and wonder why they should have such tantalizing thoughts, and if the other had had them too, and whether it would really be like that.

On her part, Emily couldn't get his burnished skin out of her mind, and the silver in his hair, and how small and perfect his feet were. She wished he would caress her arms and hands and place his tongue in the inner hollows of her elbows. She wanted to dance with him.

Chase couldn't banish her laugh from the back of his mind, the nervous flutter of her hands in conversation, her flecked eyes. He wanted to watch her lips dip into a glass of red wine and come up stained. The two of them grew more and more clumsy, dropping glasses and books and stepping on their respective pets' feet, making wreckage out of whatever was at hand.

"Whatever is the matter with you?" Chase's wife, Christina, asked after he'd ground up his third spoon in two days in the garbage disposal. It was the morning after his second dream about Emily, in which she stood laughing at him on the steps of the town library, and then slowly undressed him in a half-lit storage room.

Chase fished the mangled spoon out of the disposal and set it on the counter where it seemed to present glaring evidence as to what was wrong. If Christina had looked at him closely, she would have seen the same scratchy lines etched around his eyes, and the same nicks carved into his cheeks by an unsteady shaving hand. But she had Blake to get breakfast for, and Donovan giving her a hard time about wanting to have a friend stay over on a school night because of some science project, and the dog wanting to go out, and a plumber coming at ten. Her question had been more rhetorical than anything else.

"Will you have maintenance put up the storm windows this weekend?" she reminded him again. "There's weather blowing in."

Emily was younger than Chase by sixteen years, but she didn't seem youthful to him at all. Rather, her body did, with its matte skin and unlined, wide-open planes, but she herself did not. She seemed frail to him, uncertain and resigned about much of her life the same way that middle-aged people were.

He'd met her at an alumni fundraiser for the boarding school. She'd graduated there over ten years ago, and six years before he was ever hired. When he walked into the reception, she was standing alone at the bar, poking a straw in and out of her gin and tonic, and looking around the room. Her legs were very skinny and hair kept falling over one of her eyes. He watched her all evening. People would approach and she would converse with them, but only for a little while. He'd look over and find her sunk back in a puddle of solitude, scanning the room. He let almost the whole evening go by before he allowed himself to talk to her.

"Chase Fort," he said, giving her his hand. "Headmaster." She studied the nails. They were, she noticed, as translucent and shiny as the skins of pearls. His palm was tropically warm, like it had a tiny sun burning in the middle of it.

"Emily," she said, looking up, and then lapsed into silence. He stood next to her for a moment, his drink sweating in his other hand, until someone touched him on the shoulder and asked him about campus development. Chase left a little reluctantly, the mantle of her quiet still cloaking him. He couldn't remember the last time he'd felt an imperative to maintain silence. He hadn't known he still could.

The next time he saw her was at the Hawthorne-St. Basil's basketball game. His team, Hawthorne, was going to lose. It always did. Next to St. Basil's students, Hawthorne boys looked like the science nerds they mostly were—all geeky limbs and glasses. Even Chase could understand the urge to beat them up, to knock them around the court a little. In his heart of hearts, he really couldn't fault the St. Basil's boy who threw an elbow at one of the guards, giving him a bloody nose, and who now sat sulking on his team's bench.

Chase walked into the gym a little late. The game had already started, and he made his way along the edge of the court toward the bleachers, blinded by the lights and the new varnish on the floor, and feeling deflated by how overheated the building was. All Hawthorne buildings were too hot in the winter—the school's ancient heating system either ran full tilt or emitted nothing. After six years at the school, Chase had come to see it as a metaphor for Hawthorne's academic life. Either the three hundred boys gave everything they had, he noticed, or they just whimpered along, puffing out pathetic blasts of steam. It was the faculty's job, Chase always told them, to figure out how to get that blast of heat out of their students.

He was almost upon the mound of bleachers before he noticed Emily hunched over amid the spectators, knees to chest, arms folded, watching the game intently.

"Emily?" he said, surprised, and approached her cautiously, the way an ornithologist might sneak up on a rare bird in order to observe it. She peered at him solemnly, as if he'd just asked a painful question and she were searching for a delicate way to answer it. She was, he realized, not frail at all.

"You remembered my name?"

"It's a gift," Chase said, climbing up the benches to her. His knees ached—a new affliction of middle age. "And also part of my job. What are you doing here? I thought you lived in the city." Hawthorne was two hours outside of New York.

"My cousin Robbie," she answered, jutting her chin toward the sweating skinny boys on the court, "goes here. I thought I'd take him out for dinner."

Chase sat back, mystified. He was usually right on top of all the alumni relationships, but this one had somehow escaped his notice. Robbie Flobbler. Freshman. Stringy necked, messy room, always late for everything. Middling student.

"What do you do?" Chase asked Emily, glancing at her sideways. Her hair hung like harvest wheat along the ridge of her shoulders, veiling her. She didn't unfold her arms or straighten up to talk to him.

"I illustrate children's books," she said.

"Anything I'd know?"

"Do you read children's books?" She turned to face him. It sounded more like an accusation. Chase shifted.

"I used to. For my sons. *The Cat in the Hat. Goodnight Moon.*" He missed those times, perching on the edge of his bed with his two sons leaning in over the pages and breathing quick, absentminded children's breaths through their mouths.

"Those are good," Emily nodded. "My father used to read me *Goodnight Moon*. But my work is more modern. I do the Grasshopper Grace books."

"I haven't seen them."

"Of course not," she said. She sounded disappointed. "Why would you have? Aren't your children older now?"

"Yes," Chase said. "Fourteen and ten."

"My books are for little kids." She said it, Chase noticed, ruefully. He wondered if she were involved with anyone. He didn't see a wedding band, but that didn't mean anything these days. Perhaps she was coupled unhappily. Perhaps she merely wished for a child of her own.

He gave her his hand in parting. Again the warmth, the little sunspot in his palm. Again her fingers, long and dry like stalks of autumn grass. They held hands a little longer than protocol dictated. Then they went home and dreamed.

When they finally made love, it really was as good as they thought it would be, but neither as quiet nor as fluid as in their dreams. Chase accidentally knocked her in the ribs with his elbow when he was rolling her over, and Emily gouged his earlobe with her teeth. They would have bruises from this, Chase thought, lying next to her afterwards, marks to show. The thought alarmed him at first and then pleased him. He pictured himself mid-week at his desk, tugging on a tender earlobe and summoning up the memory of Emily's teeth. He hadn't thought yet what to say to his wife.

In twenty-one years of marriage, Chase had never before cheated, but it was a common scenario, he supposed. A good husband and father meets a younger woman and becomes a rogue. Except that he didn't feel like a rogue. Even lying next to Emily, listening to her ragged breaths in the half-darkness, he didn't long to leave his wife and family. He knew he had done something irrevocable, but he felt about it the way he felt after swimming: expanded, calmed, purged. His experience with Emily had been much the same as diving into a cold spring lake—it shocked him and numbed him, and then it woke him up. His skin felt alive, a creature of its own volition.

He hadn't meant to go to bed with her this evening, but at the same time he had. Ever since his first dream about Emily—the wicked rocking on the boat—he'd found it impossible to act normally in her presence. After the basketball game he'd seen her again at the Hawthorne winter play. Standing next to her after it, he was acutely aware of the span of her forearm extending from her rolled-up shirtsleeve, and of how clearly he could delineate the shape of her bone, long and lank, underneath the flesh. The various planes of her, the stopping and starting of them, aroused him and drew his curiosity. She inspired exploration, the desire for excavation and new discoveries. He wondered what he'd come up with—a golden statue, a jewel, a mummy's curse.

She had driven up to see her cousin Robbie play Banquo in *Macbeth*. The boy stumbled and stuttered his way through the speeches, and the play was amateur at best, but Emily hardly noticed. She was concentrating instead on the back of Chase's head three rows in front of her. The silver in his hair glowed in streaks under the stage lights, and when he turned his head she could stroke the curve of his cheek, the cant of his shoulders, with her eye. After the play she went backstage to congratulate Robbie and found Chase waiting by the dressing-room door.

"Emily," he said, startling her. His voice sounded sterner than he meant it to. It had been two weeks since the basketball game, and there were five dreams between them. There was an awkward pause.

"How is your work?" he finally asked. "Grasshopper Grace—is she catching any flies?"

She peered at him sharply. "You looked up my books?"

"Yes, well, after our conversation, I was curious. They're lovely drawings. You can find them on the internet."

She bent her head again. "You can find a lot of things on the internet, but thank you. I went to art school in Paris." His heart thudded a beat. Paris. He could imagine her there, sipping a coffee in a rattan sidewalk chair, or strolling along the Seine, a black portfolio tucked under her arm.

"Tell me about it," he said to her suddenly, his voice lowering. "Have dinner with me. I'll be in the city on Saturday. We can go anywhere you like."

She stared at his feet, considering. They were the same as in her dream—small and tucked inside newly shined loafers. He smelled like soap and starch, a clean smell that woke her, alerting her senses that something was about to happen.

"Yes," she said quickly, and they parted. This time they didn't touch hands.

He took her to an Italian bistro in the Village, a place where the food was too heavy for either of them to stomach, but it had dark corners and slow, lazy service. They picked at the food, knowing it was only a prop.

"I was engaged," she told him, "for six months. But he left me for a girl I went to primary school with. He met her at a bar. She took him home with her, and that was that."

"Are they still together?"

"I don't know. I don't really care. I'm glad we didn't get married. I don't want to be married now. I like my solitude." Her hands backed up whatever she was saying. With the word *solitude* they folded themselves in a triangle, as if to perform a pantomime for Chase. See, they said to him, we are together in our seclusion, a little knot, a fortress. We dare you to untie us.

"And your artwork?" Chase said, shifting his chair. "You like what you do?"

The hands unfolded themselves and fluttered before him like nervous birds. Yes, they told him. Unexpectedly, joyfully, yes. Her drawings matched her movements, Chase decided, delicate lines overlapping and crossing one another, tentative, each one, but hooked together in a steady armor of iron loops.

"Once I was going to be a great artist," Emily said. "Someone monumental and new. But now...," she picked up her wineglass. Her speech lapsed. "I don't paint anymore," she continued, her lips coming up from the glass stained, as Chase had imagined them. "I only do pen and ink."

"And you like that," Chase said.

"Yes. It satisfies me. It's enough. I was together once with another artist—"

"Before or after your fiancé?" Chase asked.

"After," she said, brushing the question aside brusquely. Chronology didn't matter when she was trying to make a point.

"I'm sorry," Chase said. "Go on."

"Well, I was with this artist, a painter, very talented, really. Up and coming. Anyway, the thing was, he was never satisfied. He was always working, you know? And when he wasn't working, he was worrying. Would he make it? Was he good enough? What could he do to make himself better?"

"And you don't feel that way?"

"No, never."

"What happened to the painter?" Chase asked.

"He's famous now," said Emily wistfully, "but I couldn't take it. I just wanted someone to read the paper with on Sunday. I was working with line, you see, in black and white, and everything he did was monumental, in big blobs of color."

They walked back to her apartment slowly, lingering in the winter air. She was chilly, so he gave her his scarf to put around her neck. It enfolded and warmed her, a prelude to an embrace.

They stopped in front of the stairs to her brownstone. Again, an awkward silence, but this time it was her turn for impulse.

"Come upstairs with me," she said, turning to face him.

"For a drink." Her breath caught on the edge of the sentence.

He looked up to the windows of her building. The ones on the fourth floor were dark. He wondered what was behind them.

Emily stood pigeon-toed on the stairs, wrapped in his scarf.

"I'll show you my etchings," she laughed. Chase followed her into the building and up the rickety stairs. I'll leave after one drink, he told himself. I'll sit across the room on my hands. I won't let myself kiss her.

Emily's bedroom was swathed in half-color: muted greys and whites and creams, hues that resonated on their own, but slid into one another at the same time. Chase let his eyes flit over the set of Victorian botanical watercolors on the wall. They hadn't closed the blinds, and the streetlamp bathed the room in a lurid wash of light. Chase had the sensation of floating.

"Tell me about your wife," Emily's voice said in the gloom.

"I love her," Chase answered immediately.

"Of course you do, but that's not what I asked. Tell me about her."

Chase thought. His wife was Christina, big boned and athletic and motherly. A barking laugh and hands roughened from the garden. Salty-skinned after horseback riding, apt to cry at the movies. Clever. Efficient. His partner, but perhaps not his match.

Chase had begun to feel that way about a year ago. It was middle age, he told himself, a passing time in his life. A phase. But the mind has an insidious way of casting back over memory, mining it for details. There was the time at the beginning of their courtship, for instance, when he and Christina were camping, and decided to go for a midnight swim.

"Look at the stars," he had said to her, pausing to float on his back near the edge of the small lake. "How they're reflected by the water." But Christina didn't hear him. She was gone already, set off to the other shore, intent on making it first.

"Last one there's a rotten egg," she called gaily, and so Chase lumbered after her with his awkward crawl. Why couldn't she look at the stars with him? Why was she so driven to reach the other side? He didn't like the middle of the lake. He wasn't a strong swimmer, and the inky black water made him feel vulnerable and too small for his age. He plunged his arms into the lake again and again.

Christina was waiting for him when he arrived. She grabbed him, and wrapped her arms around his neck, treading the water with her powerful legs.

"I knew you'd catch up," she said. "Look, you can see our campfire from here, through the trees. Home away from home." And then she had kissed him like some sort of water sprite.

And thus he had married her. She was capable, and he admired her for that. She shored him up and goaded him. She got him to the other side.

"Sometimes the other side is just the same as the one you were on," Emily's voice said in the half-darkness.

"Sometimes it's not," said Chase.

"Give it back!" Blake wailed as his older brother held his lacrosse stick out of reach. "Give it!" He swung a punch, but Donovan easily arched his body away from it, like a cartoon character. Donovan had gotten Chase's thick black hair and Christina's tendency to test, to push things to their limits.

"Give me ten pushups and you can have it back," he said. "On your knees!" Blake hesitated for a moment, then dropped and pumped out ten pushups, grunting at the end. He lay on the grass outside Chase's study, panting.

"You'll thank me for that, little bro," Donovan said. "Those guys are going to eat you alive." Blake was starting lacrosse in the spring and Donovan had taken it upon himself to prepare his little brother. "Now up, and I'll race you to the field house." They careened out of the line of Chase's sight, Donovan letting Blake win.

In terms of their children, Chase and Christina were split down the middle. Donovan had Chase's looks and Christina's personality, and Blake was golden and physically tough with Chase's introspective tendencies. After twenty-one years of life together, it was official, Chase thought: they were all mixed up, twisted into a Gordian knot of family relations. The only way to sever them would be right down the middle, with a blade. Telling Christina about Emily would do it. One word from him, Chase knew, and the filaments of his life would fly apart, released from all ties, but also reduced to a pile of limp threads.

Not that he wanted release. Far from it. He was happy with his family, his marriage, his work. He looked forward to his chapel talks, to running faculty meetings, to milling around the students in the halls. He loved having breakfast with the clamor of his boys percussing around him, and slipping into bed at night beside Christina. But there was also Emily and the down of baby hair at the back of her neck, the way her lips went crooked when she laughed. He closed his eyes and the half-colors of Emily's bedroom washed over him.

He'd been in the city twice since the first time they made love—once for a day trip during the week, and once for the weekend and an educational conference he didn't attend. Sometimes they spoke on the phone. Once they'd e-mailed each other. But mostly they met in dreams.

The dreams had been tempered somewhat. Now that Chase and Emily were physically involved, they no longer needed to make up what their bodies knew. Instead, they dreamed companionable things, adventures and intimacies, small journeys.

"We were drifting," Emily told him the last time they'd

been together, "down a slow Asian river. I was leaning back against you like so—" She shifted her hips in position and leaned back against him, turning the bed into a raft of bamboo poles lashed together with vines. "The banks were dense with leaves, but the sun was strong. You gave me your hat to wear. There were Buddhas peeking from the leaves. I think they were laughing at us."

"Was it the Yangtze?" asked Chase, kissing her neck. Emily shook her head, slithering her hair across his chest in a wave.

"No, nothing like that," she murmured, turning against his shoulder. "It was just some beautiful lesser waterway without even a name."

The affair continued for another two months. Sometimes Chase called her drawings up on the internet, just to have something of her near him. There was Grasshopper Grace learning to weave a web from a spider so she could catch flies. The insect was rendered with spindly legs and a bow in between her antennae. "Even though Grasshopper Grace did not have thread," the caption read, "she could still learn to spin. She would just have to find her thread elsewhere." Chase knew what happened next. He had sneaked into the children's section of the town bookstore one day and read the first book in the series.

Grasshopper Grace, wishing to rid her house of flies, goes to a spider and watches her work. She learns to spin, but, alas, has no thread. Then on the way home she makes friends with a silkworm who promises to give her his filament if she feeds him flies. She agrees, and takes him home, and they live happily ever after.

"Is everything okay?" Mrs. Chatwell had asked him, barging in at the end of his read and peering at him intently. "Can I help you find something? You're in the children's section, you know."

"Yes," Chase had answered, quickly replacing the book on the shelf. "I know. I was just reminiscing about some old times."

"Aren't your children too old for these books?" Mrs. Chatwell persisted, squinting her eyes. Chase nodded his head. Blake and Donovan read soccer magazines now—Blake comic books still. They would sneer at Grasshopper Grace offering her silkworm gentleman friend a cup of tea.

"They are, I'm afraid," Chase said to Mrs. Chatwell's crooked cardigan and creased face. "Wherever do the years go?"

"Hurrah!" Emily had crowed when he told her about the encounter. "A victory for whimsy!" She clenched her fist in the air.

"But she may tell someone," Chase mused, worried.

"She probably will," Emily agreed. "But not like you think. She'll accuse you of having some sort of breakdown or mid-life crisis. The empty-nest syndrome. She will not assume you are having an affair with the illustrator of Grasshopper Grace."

"It's not empty yet," Chase said. "That's the problem."

"I know," Emily answered, pensive.

"What are we doing?" Chase asked. "I mean, can we keep this up? Is it fair to you, to us? To my wife?"

"No, no, and no," said Emily, "but I don't want to stop."

"I don't either."

"You're in my dreams."

"I know. You're in mine." Chase took one of her hands and folded it inside his. She closed her eyes and let his skin warm her.

"Maybe they'll have to be enough," he said finally.

It was two months since Chase had last been with Emily. Shortly after the breakup he saw her at a Hawthorne lacrosse game. The air had still been chilly. They'd shaken hands. Emily was wearing gloves.

And then, six weeks later, an envelope arrived from her in the mail—a blunt, flat package the color of walnuts. It bore mysterious stamps and markings like a secret code. Chase slid it under the papers on his desk and waited until the evening study hour to open it.

Inside were copies of the illustrations for her new book, written by her as well, he noted. It was a story about a butterfly who drifts through people's dreams, and colors them. All of the pictures had delicate washes painted over them, the merest suggestions of her signature blues and pinks and greens. There was a cat flying, a child floating over a meadow, and finally, the last one, a couple on a raft sailing down a river of gleaming Buddhas. "Even lesser waterways," the caption read, "can harbor treasures."

Chase put the pictures on his desk and gazed out the window. Daytime was turning into evening, and spring was turning into summer. Insects were beginning to congregate in fierce bunches on the school's branches and stems.

"Don't forget to call maintenance about an exterminator," Christina had called to him on his way out the door this morning. "There are going to be a lot of pests this spring!"

Chase leaned back in his chair and watched a late bee drone its way home through the twilight. He'd forgotten to call the exterminator, but decided to leave off the matter for a while, his head full of silkworms and spiders and grasshoppers who knew how to weave webs. He began to tell himself a story about a lost band of ants the color of harvest wheat. Ravenous, they marched through the chambers of his heart, picking it clean.

Chase put his hand on his chest and loped across the school grounds into the vault of evening air.

"Ah well," he thought, heralding the arrival. "Let them come."

Aaron Cohen

Later that day, I was taken to the Ferris wheel.

Born in Aberdeen, Maryland, Aaron Cohen was raised in Texas, Missouri, Utah, and Florida. His short fiction can be found in *Quarterly West* and *25 & Under*. He is at work on his first novel.

AARON COHEN
It's the Least I Can Do

nniversary. Four year. Flew back to Gaines-
ville on Dad's money and here we are ladies, men, starting in
this very way, yet hesitating, perhaps like a Greyhound at the
bus stop just in case the driver with his blue sneakers hears
that wooden heel clacking on wet pavement, and a shout. A
shout. Hearing now this heel clacking on wet pavement, but
no shout, the driver tips his beat-up cigarette out the side
window, grinning, grunting, while a neatly dressed straggler
hauls himself in and pays his three-quarter toll—*clink, clink,
clink*—into the metal money well, nodding for some reason
to the officer in the first row, while taking his own green seat
in the second.

Yes, four year, *four year*, and what were Christy and I doing
but trying to go back in time, so to speak; not back four years,
but closer to seven, from Phoenix to Gainesville, to Lanyard's
Italian restaurant, where we first had met, to find, according
to Dad (Call me Dad, he says), what my life, I mean my *wife*
and I, had simply misplaced: a good strong marriage. But
instead we became the victims of another lonely old fart's
circumstances. I suddenly feel I'm being made to write on
the blackboard a thousand times *At least we're still together and
not in bloody pieces needing to be mopped off the restaurant floor like*

Glimmer Train Stories, Issue 39, Summer 2001
©*2001 Aaron Cohen*

the rest of the twenty-eight innocent people.

Bloody pieces. We were in the air for about thirty-five minutes. We should have been closer to heaven, but it was hell and more hell. The sky looked burdened with pink, angry, lumpy clouds. Christy had lost her composure about the plane's decision to jitterbug with the wind a little. I told myself not to yell, but the purpose of action is to contradict thought. *This is going to be a good day,* I kept thinking, contradicted by, "Don't be such a fuckin' *baby* all the time, Christy," while squeezing her thigh too hard. Then we were uneventfully taxi-driven by a sleepy bald man with one triangular tooth to Lanyard's. The taxi smelled of burnt popcorn and cotton candy. We didn't say two words in the car, not about popcorn, not about marriage. I wouldn't say it was always that bad.

Yes, and Dad had paid, for everything—first-class airfare, car rentals, meals, hotel suite at Holiday Inn. He was feeling so fine, as one's mood tends toward when any total stranger comes up to you and says, "Hey you, I want to buy out your entire chain of failing laundromats for three million dollars, and then, dig this, I want to turn them all into health-nut stores called Heart World. Take it and walk away, man, or tell me what I can do to win you. But no papers, none of that paper stuff. You dig."

Dad had taken it.

It was two days later—I think it was on a Sunday—that he had caught me off guard with his heightened son-in-law affection. I was mowing the backyard.

"It's crumbling," he had yelled over the noise and my shoulder. I stopped.

"Whuh?" It was as if he were talking about some kind of sand castle he'd taken years of his life to build.

"It's *crum*bling." His hand now on my shoulder, I hadn't liked that. Mower to off, black smoke going up. "I said it's *crum*bling, your *marriage,* Jimmy." Don't call me Jimmy. I spit some grass out of my mouth, but he didn't flinch.

"This," he continued, now squeezing my shoulder—never squeeze my shoulder—"has nothing do with my faith or lack of faith in you, Jimmy, but dear God, something must be done *right now*." He unfanned a brand-new map of the world and the wind immediately slapped it against his face. He flattened it on the lawn and we knelt to it.

"Now tell me. Anywhere, anywhere you want. If you could, where would you go? Not a word out of you. This is my pleasure."

"Dad, come on."

"Hit me good. I can take it."

"I don't know. I'm not into this gift thing. If you really want to know, though—"

"I do."

"Then back, all the way, *all* the way." He was laughing like a bear would laugh if a bear could. To Gainesville, I meant, and he knew it well—back to college life, the days of dreams, of heavens and hells. You could never decide which day you were in, no matter how hard you tried, but you didn't care.

"Anywhere, Jim. Come on. Pick somewhere *real*."

"You got something against my Gainesville? That's tough."

He laughed again and started scratching his ass, arched back and all. Then he tried to hug me while I started up the mower. It threw my shoulder way out of joint—the shoulder I can't move anymore, mind you.

"I love you," he said. "You ought to know that. It's the least I can do for you both." He was walking away. "She's my only daughter in the whole *world*, and that means you're my only son-in-law. We'll talk later."

We still don't know about his full angle in all this; you can never know a person's full angle. An uncle of mine once told me never to trust a nice person. The next day I found two tickets on my pillow destined for Gainesville and back. I understood what he was getting at, or maybe just a little more than before, but I still didn't trust him worth shit.

I spent the day convincing her that the tickets were really Dad's idea. She finally called him up and he explained to her that he loved her and wanted to do this one thing for her. Why he hadn't gone straight to her in the first place, God only knows. We had been watching the next-door neighbor's kids, the Finneys, when she decided we were going. The mother, Barbara, had died. And the kids hated their father. They wanted to murder him with little knives and they told me this. So we took the lot in. We felt we owed them something—her, the kids, even Mr. Finney, I guess. I have now learned this is the wrong way to handle things.

Friday. Gainesville. We were in the restaurant by 7:30. It was packed. Everyone who was still waiting for a table, including us, looked like cattle stuffed in a barn—facing all directions, stomping, itchy, wanting to be fed. It was a whiskey shoe of déjà vu if you ever knew one, with that faint floor-cleaner smell, flowers, the sauce, bread, the busyness of it all. Even the gorgeous waitresses had the same loose-fitting uniforms on. When they bent over, you could see everything noble husbands like me try so hard not to not-so-much see, but *examine*, but we end up not only *examining* but *wanting*. I've been caught red-handed, both eyes fixed, but I believe I'm still a noble husband—at least so far as this world's concerned.

Though it was far from Christmas, the smiling jazz musicians in the corner were wearing Christmas-colored plaid, thus adding to the hilarity, or rather, the clutter of it all. The guys were trying so hard to compensate for the extra crowd noise—but more importantly, for their own confidence or lack thereof as true musicians—by playing so *viciously* that I had literally noticed a new cavity.

Almost immediately, I found myself holding hands with

Christy, for support if nothing else: hers hot, mine cold, mine gripping hers, hers limp. But it was more that just holding hands, you know; it was that fear of letting go, of being the one to pull away. I had told Christy later it was a love doctor who had been sent to stitch our palms together, that we ourselves played no part in it. She *kind of* laughed. I've gotten used to that lately, this *kind-of* bullshit.

By the mere way the line was curving and formed, we were standing next to him—to Alfred, who we didn't know was Alfred, owner of Lanyard's, who we didn't know was verging on losing it. At the time, Alfred appeared to us, the observers, like some old fart (faintly resembling Dad), eating dripping garlic rolls in haste, not enjoying them and certainly not afraid of showing it. He would only eat half a roll, then put the other half on his lime-green napkin. Then he would stare at his water for a time, smelling the lemon-yellow cup, swirling the ice water around, shaking his head disdainfully. Then go back to his roll. Then start over. He was alone but appeared oblivious to this. He looked like such a run-of-the-mill old fart, too: brown slacks pulled up too high; western, white-ruffled shirt tucked in too tightly; sidewalk-grey hair flipped to the right and wetted down as if parted with a special blade. He was all starched up, too, like he was just run through the cleaners.

"Check him out."

I was playing dumb as usual.

But then her eyes dropped, and a grin washed over her face. "Look," she whispered. It was the last time I have seen her grin that great, that devious. But things are picking up.

The tie was immersed in a large bowl of tomato soup. The part of the tie which was not immersed looked wrinkled and twisty, as if he had wrung the thing out and set it back in. Five years ago, we would have laughed till snot flew, but we both agreed that, if nothing else, a good tie was being ruined here.

"Go," she said, nudging me.

"Let the poor man mind himself."

"Come *on*. You can't just leave him like that."

"He's a big boy, Christy."

Let the man find his own dead cat in the gutter, I meant to say. Yet if I hadn't eventually tapped him on the shoulder, and if Alfred hadn't looked down his Italian nose to the tie, which led like a green finger to the soup—if he hadn't looked up at me, giving me this thanks-bud smile, then taken the tie out and dabbed the tie with the dirty napkin; if a garlic roll hadn't fallen to the floor at that moment; if he hadn't put the tie back in the soup; if all these things hadn't unfolded in this specific pattern, like Dad's map—then there's a good chance me and Christy would be *dead*. Whisper the word when you say it. As this day unwinds in my mind, whoever's name, whatever single event is *the* pivot point, it's over now, *finis*, curtains drawn. The tie may have been pivotal once, but it is not pivotal now, as nothing is pivotal now, except for right now. You see, this is all so very hard to put into good words, since they enter my mind in something like hot flashes, and before I can run to the typewriter and smack the good words on the page (they hover just above the page) the hot flash is turned cold and white and empty like a new freezer or a vacated igloo, and I'm left alone and frightened, and not only is it difficult because of that, but because there is this special type of anxiety of influence I'm having: I was there, *right there*. I say anxiety because of all those antsy people who like to be called my friends who say, Now *this*, Jim, Jim, *this* is something you need to write about—not *that* or *this* or *those*. Well then, I say, how is *this*, showing him *this*, is *this* what you had in mind, or maybe *this*. Now I should, if I were smart and bound for greatness, put this in the second person, so that *you* did it all: *you* can have this wife named Christy, these problems; you can tell the old fart to take his tie out of the bleeding red soup because *your* thoughts often contradict *your* actions; lay the guilt on *you*, man.

Eventually the hostess led us to our table. It doesn't do anyone but my ego and me any good to go on about the hostess and how she was looking at me, so I'll just pass that car on the left right now. The hostess was not. Curtains drawn. She was not. A guy bases his entire life on finding the real thing, and then when he has it, the real thing turns into squash and butter and an A-1 steak every six weeks. You forget how to share. I have these theories that the young hostesses keep the faithful husband noble. My wife disagrees loudly.

We had gotten our table and ordered our food. Mushrooms and scallions for me, fettuccine Alfredo with oregano noodles (the waitress' pick on the noodles) for her. It goes back to that grass-is-always-greener rule. Christy's was so pretty and mine—so vomitous.

Let's take a tour. To your right is this couple alternating between making out with each other and their expensive martinis. There is a soldier who keeps relacing his apparently new boots. And over this small wall, two college couples, underage and drinking like squid. You are instantly reminded of yourself, caught off guard by one of the guys in particular, because he is already greying above the sideburns, like you. More important, everybody seems to be swaying, not just the squid. For a time there you feel something *stronger* than déjà vu, more real than déjà vu, as if you really *are* twenty again. But head on, which is where your head is, your view is a real zinger: a gumball machine, a cigarette machine, a round window, and the exit door. But you are two swaying catatonics. I can describe it (this odd sensation) in no other fair terms until I call up the image of how sheep in an open field might feel seconds before a tornado touches down.

Eight forty-five. Things happen pretty quickly after 8:45.

Christy occasionally glances at Alfred, but you pretend not to notice. You haven't yet asked for your check, but you can tell Christy is readying herself by the way she's squirming in her chair and trying to hide it by playing with her soup spoon, which only points you back to her squirming in her chair. You are really in the mood for something with the word "meringue" in it, but you think she wants to get back home and tell her girlfriends that Gainesville is not Gainesville anymore. But then her eyes open wide and crazy and graze your shoulder. You feel them, the creepy weight of a shadow, just about as good a feeling as a guy putting his tie back into his soup.

About half the restaurant jumps. I turn to Alfred. He is saying something in Italian, Alfred is. Soon, what he is saying is what he is spitting. Alfred bulldozes everything from the table—cup, rolls, plate, noodles from the plate, coffee and saucers, melting extra-yellow butter, salt and pepper shakers, dark red candle, bottle of expensive red wine with a black label with gold letters which (the expensive bottle) did not shatter on impact, as expensive bottles sometimes don't. I see Alfred follow someone who only he can see out the door. But he does pause, at the gumball machine, and then he's off.

Everyone picks up where they had left off. Even the soldier has returned to his lacing. The lovers smack kisses and I see part of the girl's tongue in his mouth. She has some martini in her hair; the young man is trying to wipe it off without her noticing, but he has some in his hair, too. A busboy starts sweeping up the spill Alfred made, as if this were all routine (which we found out later it is, it was). The cash register rings. The crisis is over. Tuck in the kids, everybody, time for bed. The jazz starts up again playing "Singing in the Rain." The hostess is not looking at you, or I mean me. Alfred is gone, but he is not gone.

"Now, you," I say, "you can't tell me some meringue right now doesn't want to be *rolling* down your tongue and down, down, down your pink throat into that pretty tummy of yours. Lemon meringue chilled pie. Sparkling pie, fresh pie. Come on, why have you got to look so sour-faced all the time."

"Honey, I'm just thinking. Can't a woman think a little?"

"Sorry."

"Jim, are you ever in a good mood?"

"Why?"

"I mean a *really* good mood."

"I'm always in a good mood. Why?"

"I mean a really, *really* good mood."

"What's your point, Christy? Please don't say you want a divorce. I'm too young to have a divorce. Divorces are for people with kids." I look at the ceiling and start talking in tongues to it. And I get her to laugh.

Alfred bulls his way back in through the exit door. All sights and sounds are exaggerated. He seems swollen, Alfred does, flat out of breath, too. One eye is open too wide. He's smiling, all three teeth in good standing. Alfred is at the gumball machine. I'm clenching my fork, not for the sake of the meringue anymore, either. Christy turns around, and Alfred says something to her in Italian and then blows her a kiss. I stand. Christy humors him. A hostess plucks my elbow and says to sit down, please, just *have a seat, sir*. I try to eat some now-cold mushrooms but out of the top part of one eye I see the gumball machine crash into the cigarette machine, into little bits. The machine drops. Glass flies. Red, blue, green, yellow, and white gumballs, my least favorite, spread.

Alfred says something as he pushes an older couple who's leaving out the door, and I can see the woman tumble into the street crying, "Oh, Carmichael, where *are* you!"

I think by this time, in the tradition of accurate American

slang, one may say Alfred had officially lost it. And I remembered so well my childhood, all the movies, all the books, all the friends. I had a good life. Alfred's eyes were set deep inside him and he looked excited if not flat-out electrified. That's when he pulled out the gun, of all things.

For about five really good and two real bad reasons, I want to interrupt myself to tell you about Barbara Finney's death, and just why we feel so sorry for the Finneys now, over here. It's a small, inner story, a balloon inside another balloon. Very unfair, but right now I don't give a damn.

The first year we moved into Winter Springs our own Barbara Finney, with the flowing strawberry-blond hair that my wife had so much envied ("You *must* tell me your secret"), and her three kids, Evan, Robin, and Chris Finney, went to the annual County Fair. They had invited us and we had gone, reluctantly and in separate cars, but we had gone. The price was a little steeper for the Finneys that year than for the rest of the world. It was about nine at night when it happened. Things were clearing out, and Barbara kept nagging me and Christy to go on Inside Out (a fitting enough name for the ride that claimed in so many words to turn your skin around) with her and the kids.

"You'll just *love* it."

Inside Out was one of those rides made in the late sixties, early seventies, that somehow skipped inspection every year. Flipped your ass up and back, shot you straight up, then dropped you, saving your knees from bowing and splitting by twirling you like a baton at the last minute ... in a nutshell, of course, that was what Inside Out was all about. Understandably, it was the most popular ride in the universe.

Well, Barbara Finney had nice enough kids, she was a nice enough adult, et cetera. The ride didn't know any of this. Christy and I had chickened out at the last minute.

"We'll meet you by the soda stand."

They never did. Barbara had had her long flowing hair up that day, like a Hare Krishna. About five minutes into everything, the ride gaining speed, whirring, people screaming, wind blowing, howling, the ride doing its job well—that long flowing hair had gotten caught inside one of the many whirling parts just beyond the cage. Somehow—somehow is the key word. Jesus. The thing had somehow snatched up her whole healthy scalp while approaching that terminal velocity one might call the actual thrill. And the ride kept on whizzing and spinning and *roaring* until the control-panel operator saw a single drop of blood on the back of his own hand. Looked like somebody had exploded when we finally got there.

Anyway, Chris Finney, the youngest of her children at nine, the one who was sitting in the same gondola as his mother, understandably does not remember a thing. But then again, his mouth doesn't move anymore. The accident happened to the Finneys, the people next door. And we? We canoed ahead, a little shaken, but more or less still sitting by the fire and HBO, eating cold Pop-Tarts in the dark while Christy's fingers walk and slide up my leg, and I for some dark reason keep pushing them away. We're giggling a little less, but the people next door are not giggling at all. I tell you this in all seriousness. Life is not a riddle to find out who deserves what.

A *gun*, did I say? Shit, it's something a guy like me rarely ever sees, and when he does it's behind that special glass casing. I don't hunt. I'm not a sporting man. In fact, besides a few skeet-shooting lessons in middle school, I don't think I've ever held anything but a .22. I imagine they're heavy and stiff and fun as hell to shoot. I suppose there's quite a kick and a rush when shooting a good strong gun, one that could kill a mountain goat, or even your stepmother. There were no big wars during my time, so playing with guns wasn't permissible. Seeing the gun, then, was fantastic, mystifying, and horrifying, like a lion out of his cage.

Christy was nearest him when the first shot went off. The people still standing started pouring out the door, and most of

the employees, too. It was the loudest thing I ever heard in my life—the shot, the screams, the people, a tremendous and cohesive roar. Almost automatically, she and I were under the table. The jazz had stopped and my heart was doing wonderful things inside me, foaming, I think. Christy's mouth was on my shoulder and she was breathing through my shirt for some reason, slobbering.

My father left my mother when I was fifteen—never saw him again except in pictures. My mother remarried this Rick guy whose brain *is* a nutshell. She told me that if I couldn't carry on a normal adult conversation with him, it was certainly my choice in the matter, but then it would be her choice not to speak to me until I straightened my tie and sucked in my hate.

This all doesn't exactly make me a hero either—I know that, you know that. Hiding under the table like that was not a sign of fearlessness—disowning my mother, not wanting to know my father, wanting the hostess to look at me when I was trying to reconcile relationships with my life, I mean my wife, was not glorious. But I've written these words as genuinely as anyone in my boat and with my carefully sculpted personality can; not two cents of it is horse piss as far as I'm concerned. That doesn't mean I'm not making this *my* story, and not the people who need this to be their story, who can't make it their own, those twenty-eight people who are dead. And the whole baby thing that I haven't explained. I could have easily broken Christy's hold to get to her, now that I think about it.

I remember hearing Christy's almost orgasmic breathing. The lights were out. The baby, I heard the baby—the baby screaming from far away and Alfred talking to her in goochy-goochy-goo language. I tried to jerk away.

"*Don't leave me.*"

Her fingernails were inside my arm now. At a certain point the beer pitcher above us had exploded. But I was not exactly struggling like a madman in a straightjacket then, or when I heard the baby. An old, spotty hand came under the table.

There was a silence. Christy was yanked from my grip, stiff. I cowered farther under that table, passing out.

I didn't bring a typewriter under that table, so obviously we got out, unhurt. But that doesn't mean we weren't hurt. When the police came—and yes, they had come within five minutes—they were most cautious about the gumballs on the floor. Alfred was found sitting at a table with his nose bleeding. He had apparently tried to rape my wife, but she had kneed him in the face, breaking seven separate bones, and then she darted out, vomiting, she said. Alfred was lighting a match when the cops entered. I was still under the table, my voice dead. I had come to, but was still swaying.

Gumballs were arranged in some alien pattern on the table, but I must not have seen that until later. Oh yeah, and Alfred had this tic in his face. Twenty-eight of them—the soldier, the hostesses, the young grey-haired dude, two of the jazz players, and the newlyweds or whoever they were. Tabitha Mitty at eight, dead with a Teddy bear under her dress, apparently to protect it. A special service later. I had given the speech to about ten thousand people. You were not there.

The baby lived, was found on one table, lying there sleeping, pacifier in mouth now, tomato sauce on dress. Her folks had run off in such a hurry. Had they forgotten their own daughter? They never made it out. The dad was slumped over the back of a chair, the mom was lying on her stomach near some military man, a big hole in her back.

Before we were ushered outside, somehow the cops screwed up about cuffing him. Somehow, somehow. We were both standing by our table, mesmerized, unfocused, as if we were murdered, too. Three cops were standing by us. Seven were escorting Alfred out. He still had on his green Polo tie, though it was now flung over one shoulder like he had just gotten off a motorcycle.

He walked by me, laughing, looking me straight in the eye. He had a free hand, and he made that free hand into the shape of a gun, and he put that shape on my shoulder.

"Was it fun for you?" he said.

Then he moved his thumb like a trigger. I heard a boom. I haven't been able to move my arm since. Of course, my doctor says it will wear off. It's all in here, he says, patting my head, then my belly. I still can't move my arm. There's still feeling, but, Doctor, when I try to wiggle my pinky I get a thick feeling in my stomach, and I'm back in the restaurant with Alfred's eyes upon my face. It's almost as if it were my penalty for basing my life on the past. "Now what window do you look out when you're driving your car down the road, Jim?"

"The back one?" The doctor doesn't laugh, but does smile.

We're still together, not necessarily better, but changed. We are both getting help. Slow down, rest, have sex, eat celery with the tips dipped in peanut butter, and keep buying Pop-Tarts, and don't toast them. But I know this is the wrong way to end it, to do it, so I fear it, but at the same time cannot control it. I mean, I want to talk to you all night about how Christy is, and how I *need* her now more than ever, but I see him, and you see him, and the bus driver sees himself.

The bus driver. He is driving slowly as he cranes his neck behind him, seeing his wife with a wrinkled shirt and the child that needs a haircut, both sound asleep. Quiet. How did they get there? The bus driver rounds the corner and ahead sees the bus station, and when he pulls into the bus station parking lot and slides into space 192, he turns off the engine, goes over to the sleepy heads he calls his family, pulls up his pants a little, then nudges them both with his good hand, whispering, *Time to get up.* But they don't. They don't. So he edges out another cigarette from his tight back pocket. *A moment more of silence won't hurt.* Expecting to find the cigarette beat up like the others, he is surprised when it is not. It is bleach white, no dimples, no bends, no wrinkles, a new-born smoke protected somehow, as if inside a bubble. All equally crushed by the man's ass, but one.

CHARLES BAXTER
Writer

Interview

by Linda B. Swanson-Davies

*Charles Baxter, who teaches at the University of Michigan in Ann Arbor, has written short-story collections (*A Relative Stranger, Through the Safety Net, Believers, Harmony of the World*), novels (*Shadow Play, First Light, The Feast of Love*), and a collection of essays on fiction,* Burning Down the House. *His work is regularly anthologized and has won numerous prestigious awards and grants.*

Charles Baxter

I had to laugh when I was rereading the interview you did with Stewart Ikeda in which you said, "Most of my own large-scale insights have turned out to be completely false." There are many places in your fiction and in your book of essays, Burning Down the House, *where you seem to focus on reality versus wishes or imagined insights. It seems to me that fooling ourselves a little bit can either be very disruptive, or it can help us cope, or even flourish. In raising your son, have you tried to offer any particular perspective on that issue?*

What a good question. What a hard one to answer. I have always been very leery of offering him what I would call abstract advice. If you offer young people abstract advice, you begin to sound like a blowhard or like Polonius in *Hamlet*, and so usually the advice that I've given him has been extremely practical in particular situations. A friend of mine told me that his father had given him one piece of advice about women, for example, and the advice was, women will forgive you if you're too fast, but they won't forgive you if you're too slow.

Huh.

I would never say a thing like that.

No. That is an amazing thing. But this is what your friend's father picked to tell him. Has that shaped your friend's life at all?

I don't think it has, but I think we're all so suspicious now of general, blanket, ethical claims that we are—or I should say I am—very, very slow to issue those sorts of dogmas in my own life and to my own son. I just don't do it. If he had misbehaved more than he has, I might have had to resort to them, but he's been a good kid, solid citizen, fine young man. When that happens, you don't have to start declaring laws and commandments. You just don't.

My daughter has always been a very sensible and good-hearted kid and so I've never had a need to—nor an ability to, since she's been very independent from the start—tell her what to do. But I have told her a million things, a million things. Because when I was growing up I felt like I didn't know enough. Oh, that reminds me of when your character Bradley said that his parents had not told him, taught him, anything of value.

Yeah, well, he's in a bad way in that scene. His second wife has left him for a man she's always loved, although she hasn't admitted that to herself. He's been set adrift, and he's gotten into his car, and he's gone to a tourist attraction in Michigan. Everywhere he looks, he sees people kissing, and he thinks there's this vast conspiracy of romance that he hasn't been invited to. He's in that situation that lonely people sometimes find themselves in of thinking that everybody else must know a secret that they haven't been told. How else could they have these happy relationships? How else could they find one another?

You know, when you're unhappy in the way Bradley is unhappy in that scene, you think, Somebody should have told me how to deal with this, and nobody did.

As though there were *a way to deal with it.*

As though there were a way to deal with it. I noticed in the airport this morning when I was looking at mass-market glossy magazines, there are two words that appear on the covers of those magazines with great regularity. One, of course, is *sex*. But the other word is *secrets*. That is, if you buy this magazine you will learn the secret to sex. That plays into this idea that other people have been told a secret truth that has been kept from you. Bradley simply thinks, It was my parents, they never told me what I was supposed to know.

Titles. Do they come to you, or do you think them up? What purpose do you think they serve?

Sometimes a story can do perfectly well without any specific title. You don't remember the title for very long and it doesn't matter. But with some stories, the title is extremely impor- tant. One of my stories in *A Relative Stranger* is about an old woman who tells her husband stories while he's in an as- sisted-care facility. She tells him stories about their lives to- gether. Some of these stories are real, and some of them are made up. She's making up these stories in order to invigo- rate him. That story is called "Scheherazade" because I wanted to tap into the idea, which is imbedded in the structure of the *Thousand and One Arabian Nights*, that Scheherazade tells stories in order to keep death at a distance.

With my book *Believers*, the title is quite important because all of the stories in that book are about moments in which a character chooses to believe or not to believe in something that he or she has been told or that *seems* to have happened. I've had titles changed on me. My first novel had a different title, but my agent and editor said, You can't use this title. My second novel had a different title than the one it eventually had. It's now called *Shadow Play*.

Oh, yes, right, and it was Leavings?

It was *Leavings*, and the editors said this is a very distasteful title and nobody will want to buy a book called *Leavings*.

Do you believe that?

I didn't think so then. I think it's possible now. It is true when I've told this story to some people, they've said, Yeah, you know, it does sound like what mice leave behind in the kitchen. But at the time, I didn't think it was a bad title.

I still like it.

I thought it had all of the associations that I wanted for that book. The newest one, *The Feast of Love*, is a title that I've always had for that book. Just always had it right from the start.

So you knew where you were going.

I knew where I was going with it. I didn't know how I was going to get there, but I always knew that the book thematically was going to be about love.

You mentioned in Burning Down the House *how different the possible outcomes are when a character experiences desire versus longing. When you are writing a story, I wonder, do you already know what feelings the characters will have, or do they reveal themselves as you go?*

It's both. Sometimes I know what the characters will want and I watch them as they act out the results of having that feeling. But if the story seems to be too cool, or flat, I'll have to put something in the story to heat up the character to make the desires or the longings stronger than they are, so that the character will act out in some interesting way. Act, or act out.

But I don't always know these things ahead of time. What I try to do is just see the scene, to daydream my way through it, and then to make it plausible by giving the character enough features of characterization so that *that* person would do *that* thing.

Do you ever suggest that your students look at particular words that they've chosen?

Oh, certainly. Sure. Sometimes a story will stand or fall on a simple word choice or on one sentence in the middle of a paragraph that either says too much or doesn't say enough. It either takes us too far or doesn't take us far enough. I am amazed by the way that a story can fail by having a few words out of place. More often than not, I think it's because the writer has been afraid of turning the heat up. He or she—the writer—has found a situation or a feeling and been afraid to face it down, and so the language goes a little dead. The scenes go a bit dead and you think: this story isn't facing up to all the consequences that it set into motion.

Right. It does make all the difference in the world: whether the author is committed to going or not. In Burning Down the House, *you said that all moralizing implies some knowledge of the future. Do you think that we are doing more moralizing these days because we would like to imagine we had a little bit more knowledge of the future?*

I think it comes from a number of sources. It's difficult to talk about it; it's a large question.

And it's kind of upon us now. Perhaps in retrospect it will be clearer.

Well, it's upon us now partly because of the fallout and the consequences of what Phillip Roth called the Monica Lewinsky spring and summer, and our interest, not to say our fascination, with the love lives and the behaviors and misbehaviors of public figures. I think one of the reasons we worry about these matters is that many people don't have the same traditional set of religious values and guides for behavior that they once did. So you look around and you start to ask yourself what the governing principles that people should be following are. And the answer is, probably there aren't any, unless we can all agree on them. Or a lot of people can agree on them—but there's a big difference between *a lot* and *all*.

When people aren't sure how they should behave, and how other people should behave, you get a lot of moralizing. You get public figures standing up on TV and saying, This is what people should be doing. It's an odd time in our history. I've read three novels lately that have dealt with this subject: J. M. Coetzee's novel *Disgrace*, Francine Prose's book *The Blue Angel*, and Roth's *The Human Stain*, they're all about shame. They're not love stories, they're shame stories.

What a trying time.

No, it's a good time in fiction. But it is also a time when writers and readers are interested in shame and where it comes from and how it is deployed in public life.

So something good may come of it in the end.

Something may.

I think the answer is probably no to this question: Do commercialism and power fit into the moralizing, again, as though we are taking some control of our lives? You talk a lot about commercialism. You obviously are terribly conscious of it.

I want to answer your question sensibly. And I want to be mindful about the power of commerce and commercialism in relation to what we're talking about. But it's hard to fit them together, because commerce basically doesn't do anything except to tell us to want products and to buy them. That's what a commercial society does. It produces products for our appetites, for profit. If there's going to be a source of models of behavior, it has to come from somewhere else. You're not going to find out how you should act from TV commercials, or a TV show, either.

I had an agreement with my daughter this past summer. She wanted to move into an apartment during summer break rather than come back home. I said I would pay her rent if she didn't buy any clothes or watch television at all the entire summer.

Oh, what an interesting—how did you know that she'd honor it?

She's absolutely trustworthy.

What did she say?

First she said, "Sure!" Then she said, "Not any? For how long?" Then she said, "Why?" Anyway, it was an interesting experiment. She did do it. I just wanted her to experience a small chunk of life without the constant bombardment of TV or the hunt to buy the things that our culture says a person needs.

Yeah, yeah.

David is one of the harder-to-like characters in The Feast of Love.

David and Diana are both hard to like.

Diana, I felt for more. I don't know why. But I did.

Oh. A number of readers have said that it took a long time for them to warm to Diana, that they thought that she was one tough cookie.

Oh, she was. There's no question. It's just that I think I believed what she said about herself, which I'll ask you about a bit later. So David had admitted… he didn't say to himself, "I like to hunt," he rather was a hunter and that simplified his identity. He didn't really have to consider the matter at all. It amazed me that throughout that entire book, you were able to get people to make self-disclosures that were so amazing—I don't really understand why it worked so well. I wouldn't usually believe a story where you have somebody telling intimate things about themselves that they'd rather not even know. How did you do that?

I imagined for myself a scene—let's say a bar around eleven-thirty at night, it's getting late. You know, the fans are rotating in the ceiling. Most of the people have gone, and someone is sitting there, telling me things that are amazing and true. The way that an old friend may sooner or later open up to you and tell you some feature of her life that you've always suspected but waited years to hear from her. I think in stories and novels we often wait for that moment, signature statements, signature actions. David saying, "It wasn't that I hunted, I was a hunter. That was my essence. That was what I did. And in some sense it's still what I do." I think it's wonderful when characters open up themselves because it's as if something that has been hidden has bubbled up to the surface and—because it's been hidden—it's a treasure. And you've waited to hear it.

Oh, certainly true. I am not a writer myself and so I look at it and I think, how did that work? I was terribly impressed.

The way it works, in this novel at least, which has a slightly unusual form, is that the characters are confiding in someone. At first it's a shadowy figure named Charlie Baxter, but gradually they're confiding in the reader.

Right. Yes, it's terribly, terribly personal.

It's very personal, but it's also dramatic. They're telling you stories. They're telling you about what happened to them.

Do you feel like this is really one of your masterpieces, thus far?

Oh, it's not for me to say. It's not for me to say. Every time I'm working on a book I'm hopeful and my expectations are high, but at the same time, I'm practicing steely detachment. So that, if things don't go well, I won't suffer unduly. I think it's important for writers not to become grandiose about what they've done.

I agree, I sure agree. But I do think it's a marvelous book. Okay, Chloé. Oh, dear, I think I'm going to remember to put that accent on there.

You're gonna say Chloe.

Yes, I am. It's too hard.

Well, even I slip back into saying Chloe sometimes, but it is Chloé. It's customized.

She's customized. She and Oscar were such an incredible pair in that they remained, to me, deeply innocent. They're the kind of kids I would take home and put up for a few weeks, you know? Despite all kinds of evidence to the contrary—particularly the sex-for-pay thing. I mean, that's out there.

But even that is rather innocent of them.

I know. I know.

They think they can get through it without anything happening to them.

Is that an element of innocence?

Partly. You think that what you're doing is not going to have terribly large consequences. If you're *not* innocent, you know that there's going to be a bill that's going to arrive.

Because you will have had a background of not-innocence and you will have seen results already.

Exactly right.

I wondered, too, if it had something to do with the defamiliarization that you talk about in Burning? *Looking at things through a different lens to see more what a thing really is rather than making it a symbol and then skipping over it.*

Well, with Chloé, the first reaction most readers will have, I thought, would be here's this young woman, only about nineteen or twenty, and she's infatuated with this guy Oscar. Oscar's infatuated with her. They're not going to be anything more than comic relief in this book. We don't have to take her seriously, partly because she seems to be flighty. Partly because she's innocent, and partly because we generally don't take young people like this especially seriously. But what if you defamiliarize things a bit? What if it turns out that they actually know something, the two of them? About real passion that the other characters in the novel only dimly understand. What if it's Chloé and Oscar who look like nitwits at first, who really have got the secret to something? What if you write it that way? So that's what I did.

It certainly worked. I think you're right about how easy it is to dismiss a girl in a coffee shop, who's dressed a little silly and talks funny. We do it all the time.

Do it all the time. We don't pay any attention to those people, but the whole point of fiction is to make us pay attention. To bring our attention in a society full of distractions back to people we wouldn't have noticed otherwise.

Right. In real life. Is that one of your goals when you're writing fiction? Do you want to change me, as a reader? Or is this once again an area that you won't tread into?

Only insofar as I would like you to take the story away with you in your head, to remember it and conceivably to recognize part of your own life in the story, and to recognize the story in part of your own life. So that someday it may happen that you will be in the situation and you'll say, This is a little bit like one of Charlie's stories. In the way that people say, My God, this is like a Hitchcock movie.

Right. Right! Not very often but—

Not very often, and it's not necessarily the kind of experience you want to have, but one of the characteristics of art is to color our experience so that it begins to look or to feel like something we once saw in a book or a movie or a painting. You know? When you're walking downtown now, sometimes you'll say: that coffee shop looks like a Hopper painting. That's what art can do. It can give you a frame of reference for certain kinds of experiences.

Kind of thickens our lives up.

Right.

When you won the Lila Wallace Reader's Digest Award, if I understand correctly, that committed you to community service. You said back in that earlier interview that you could not yet judge what impact it had had upon you. And I wonder now, several years later, if you can.

The grant or the community service?

The community service.

It had an impact. I realized in a way I hadn't before how many communities of writers there are in this country. How many people there are who are eager to tell stories or to get down their histories or history that they know. And to what degree it's true that we still live, despite all of the media hype, in a print culture. I know there's a lot of publicity that's out there that says that print culture is dying. There's a fair amount of evidence that our lives are being changed a great deal by what we see on screens. But what I discovered, on this Lila Wallace grant, was that in all these little communities where I was going, there were many, many people who wanted to write, who wanted to have fellow writers reading their work and to help them along, and that there wasn't a community *without* people like that.

Wow. That must have impressed you substantially.

It did impress me. I'd be happy to know that they were also active readers. I couldn't always be sure that they were. It can be worrisome if all the people you talk to who say they want to be writers also say, "I don't read." That's like saying, "I'd like to be an electrician, but I don't know much about wires."

We know, by comparing the number of subscriptions we have to the number of manuscripts that we get in, that there are many people who want to write but don't realize the importance of reading. I think sometimes beginning writers in particular don't realize how much reading will help them to refine their own work; they just know how badly they want to get their stories out, which I can understand.

There's a certain stage of writing that comes out of self-involvement and narcissism. If you're going to become serious as a writer at all, you have to get beyond that, so that you are concentrating less on yourself, and more on the writing and the story. You simply have to move yourself out of the way. Even if you're writing a memoir. You have to think at least as much about the language as your own history. You have to think about the way in which the story's being told.

And that's hard for people who are motivated by the need to get it out.

That's true. That's true. They have every right to say, I have a great story and I'm going to tell it any way I can. So tell it any way you can, but then go back over it and think about what you can do to it to make it more effective.

Think about its life.

Right. Right. An actor does not go on stage in order to have emotions. An actor goes on stage in order to convey emotions to the audience.

And they use what they have available to do that. If you were going to tell a new writer to go back and look at their words, which kinds of words would you tell them to look for?

Nouns and verbs. And cut the adjectives, unless they absolutely had to have them. Make sure the verbs are the very best ones that you can find. Make them direct. Make them forceful. Make them to the point. If the tone of the scene requires a slightly unusual verbal texture, use your thesaurus. Use the dictionary. Vladimir Nabokov said that a writer who didn't spend time just paging through the dictionary looking for good words was not a real writer. I think when stories rise to a moment of great tension or release or traumatic revelation, the language is absolutely crucial, and you have to make sure that the emotional temperature of the language matches the emotional temperature of the scene. Of course it's possible to have a highly charged emotional scene that is narrated in completely flat and affectless language, and that can work once or twice, but it won't work all the time.

Right. I've a story right here that we're rejecting today—it's compe-

tently written and you can tell that the story is very full, but the writer isn't letting us into it, almost as though he is protecting himself from its power. But if the author won't go there, the reader can't either.

Right, right, right. The language is meant to transport and if it doesn't, it's failed.

You seem to have a huge picture in your head that incorporates all kinds of big cultural and historical issues that influence writing. I'm very impressed by your ability to weave it all together in your mind. You were talking about Americans' love of epiphany and dislike of silence, of the sort of life circumstances that encourage melodrama; that there's a trend toward irony in German writing. I guess I'd like to hear a little bit about those actual ideas, but also I'd like to know if you have a feeling for how your brain is organized that you can do that. I mean, I can almost picture it, the head of an idea needling through your brain, picking up applicable threads and coming out with a nicely developed theory.

Well, you know, Henry James said about writers that they should be people on whom nothing is lost. That's much too hopeful. There's a great deal that's lost on me, that I don't understand. All I try to do is to observe people in their behaviors so that I can use them, use what I've learned, in my stories. I try to pay attention to the way people speak and act, and when somebody says something to me that bothers me, or behaves in a way that I don't understand, I will simply try to think through why that happened. Because I've been on tour with *The Feast of Love*, and because I'm now getting reviews of the book, I've been thinking about the reactions that some people have had to it.

One of the things I've noticed is that in the generation of people who are in their twenties and early thirties, the word "love" is almost embarrassing, and I've been trying to think about why. One interviewer said to me, You don't really think, do you, that people talk about love anymore? She was about twenty-five.

There was another review of *The Feast of Love*, in a little magazine called the *Barcelona Review*, which said that the title was "dreadful." And the reviewer went on to say that it's a dreadful title because no one, neither a man nor a woman, would dare carry a book with the title *The Feast of Love* onto the subway. The sense of it being that it's too old fashioned, it sounds like a romance novel. I don't know how my mind is organized. All I know is that at various times in my life I have certain preoccupations, certain things that I can't help thinking about. And right now I can't help thinking about why it may be the case that we've come to a point, culturally, where a title like *The Feast of Love* could be embarrassing to people.

So that's what I'm trying to think through. Whether it's because we have a culture of irony now and of cool emotional responses... A writer named Vivian Gornick, who wrote a book called *The End of the Novel of Love*, argued that people don't expect love to supply the meaning of their lives anymore, and they don't read novels about love in order to find that kind of meaning. It's an interesting idea that I think may very probably be wrong, but it's an interesting idea all the same. These questions have a lot to do with the kinds of stories people tell. And the kinds of stories they want to read or think about. I mean, it's one thing to say you shouldn't be talking about love in an abstract way. But it's another thing if you're teaching a class and someone comes in and says you can't write this kind of story anymore. Nobody will read it; no one will care about it. It's not intellectually viable. So these are not just literary questions. Literary questions spill out into cultural matters, into theoretical matters. They're all connected.

How did you get as much knowledge as you have of history? Did you major in it or did you just pay better attention than I did?

I was not a very good student in history classes, but I think anyone who worries about where a particular idea or set of behaviors originated, where it came from, will start to worry or think about history. Where does this come from? Where does that come from? How do I find out how this beauty or this weirdness came into existence?

Do you have ideas about trends in writing that you think we might be moving toward now? For instance, you talked a lot about how everyone wants an epiphany at the end of the story now.

When he was an old man, the composer Virgil Thomson was asked where he thought music was going, and Thomson replied, I don't care where it's going, I want to know where it's just been. You're tempting me to become a prophet of sorts. I know that recently we have been through a period of fiction in which there's been, for a lot of reasons, a great deal of attention paid to abusive behavior and to shame. You have to ask yourself if you have [social] trends that lead to stories about abusive fathers, abusive relationships, stories that are very concerned with obsessive-compulsive or addictive behaviors. I'm sure you see stories like this coming into *Glimmer Train* all the time.

What is the next stage after that going to be? I don't know. And I think a person really risks looking like a fool.

I didn't mean to invite you to do that.

Oh, no, but you see I *wish* I knew. I wish I knew. I would like to say, Oh, the kinds of stories that I'm writing would be the sorts of stories that we may see next, but I have absolutely no certainty of that. I don't know whether I'm in a vanguard or a rearguard. Whether I'm at the front or the middle or the back.

We never do know, do we?

No.

We get in a fair number of stories that don't have a lot of depth or resonance. How would you suggest writers look at their work to discover and address those things?

There are about five questions you can ask yourself about

stories, and they're not foolproof, but they're useful. One is, what do these characters want? Second is, what are they afraid of? Third is, what's at stake in this story? Fourth is, what are the consequences of these scenes or these actions? And the last one is, how does the language of this story reflect the world of the story itself?

Now, if a writer is writing a story and looks at you and says: I don't know what my characters want. I don't think they want much of anything. Then the story is in trouble. If you don't know what's at stake in the story, it means that nothing stands to be gained or lost in the course of it. Something has to be risked. The characters have to want something or to wish for something. They have to be allowed to stay up past eleven o'clock and to make mistakes. If there's a flaw that many beginning writers have, it is that their characters don't risk enough. They are just sitting in chairs having ideas. I had a student a few months ago, when I was in residency at a university, who said, I don't want my characters to do anything, I just want them to think through the problem of nature versus culture.

That's not exactly a story, is it?

That's what I tried to tell her. But she was determined to write a story about issues. I mean, this is an old thing to say, but if you want to write something about *issues*, write an essay. That's what essays are for. If you want to see the consequences of ideas, write a story. If you want to see the consequences of belief, write a story in which somebody is acting on the ideas or beliefs that she has. But that's why it's important to have a sense of what your characters want.

There are some wonderful sentences in Feast. *I had some favorites: when Bradley says, "I'm a king and not a leaf." Then Harry sending off his letter to his terribly dysfunctional son: "In the dark it lay among the fellow letters, whispering to one another their messages of love and longing and betrayal." And Diana with her statement: "On some days I'd like to be more like Chloé, who has star quality. But I'm not like her, and I won't be. I'm bad because I lack useable tenderness, and I don't have a shred of kindness, but I am not a villain and never have been. That's what you should re-member about me." Do you remember writing those particular words?*

I remember writing the line about the envelopes talking to each other in the mailbox.

How did you come up with that?

I'd been driving around that day and I had written a couple of paragraphs of Harry's chapter, and I was just imagining the envelope falling into the mailbox, and I thought, you know, it's a little community of letters down there. What if the let-ters talk to each other? What if we had objects that were suddenly alive? And I remember the line about Bradley being a king because that was a particularly difficult chapter to write. It was difficult because Bradley is drifting through his household. His first marriage has broken up; his second mar-riage hasn't arrived on the scene yet. If you have a character who's feeling melancholy you need to, I think, temper it in some way with humor or some kind of spice. In Harry's case, well, this is a common enough male fantasy, and so I do re-member writing that sentence too. Most of my time behind the keyboard, I'm in an almost half dream state, and I do not remember writing most sentences. I remember writing the section that you read about Diana, because I thought it was important to address the reader. I knew perfectly well that a lot of readers were not going to like her. I knew that Diana would know that she's not especially likable, and that the point about Diana is not likability. That's never been the point of that woman.

What is her point?

Strength. Getting what she wants, not admitting to herself what's she feeling until the last minute, being smart and being verbal, arguing with people—that's why she's a lawyer—until she makes her case.

I was also moved by Esther's offering to Chloé. "'Here,' Esther said, and she pulled a green bracelet off her arm and put it on Chloé's. 'What is it?' the girl asked. 'Malachite. It gives courage.'" I imagined Esther, like her husband, believes that she has a rational view of the world, which may be mistaken, but it's so clear that— bottom line—she does not care about that in any way. And it just struck me that reason and love don't necessarily spend a lot of time together.

Not necessarily, and when you're reassuring somebody, ideas will only take you so far. At a certain point you really have to pull out something ritualistic or magical that will get you through, and Esther knows Chloé well enough to know that she's the sort of young woman who needs that kind of stuff around her.

But Esther was wearing it herself. Part of her must surely believe in it herself.

Well, just because you're a research chemist doesn't mean that you don't believe in the power of a bracelet to give you courage.

True. The word faith came up for me when I was reading both of these books and I wondered if that has any resonance for you as well.

Well, it has to have resonance for me if I'm writing a novel about how people are paired off and whether they believe that they're going to stay together or not. Belief and faith are connected in the sense that Chloé has the belief, which is close to a faith, that Oscar is going to reappear on the scene somehow. Diana and David have the belief that they're matched. They don't have faith, because they're not like that. It wouldn't do to say all characters have faith, because they don't. But you know when you're writing stories you're also thinking about how these people are going to end up. What is the future going to hold? And when you speculate about the future, you're thinking about belief. You believe that certain things are going to happen, or you have faith that there will be certain outcomes. Faith is related to evidence of things not seen. And what is not seen, in part, is the future, and what's going to happen to us. That's why I think about faith in relation to story telling.

I saw a movie the other night that someone had recommended. I was affected in some of the ways that she was, but mostly I was destroyed by the violence involved in it. It was hideous, and it shook my confidence in my own beliefs to some degree—it's really important to me that I be able to look at people and believe—as I do—that there is, you know, a spark of light in all living things, that there's hope for us to improve ourselves by tending that spark. Anyway, it kind of shook me, momentarily at least, and I wondered what kind of things shake you. It is a personal question, and you may or may not be okay with that. What sort of things shake you, and how do you regain your own equilibrium?

Oh, I suppose, since I'm an American, that the things that shake me up are violence and cruelty. A kind of large-scale acceptance of violence and the idea that violence is inevitable and necessary. It also shakes me up that we may be beginning—I hope we're not, but that we may be beginning—to accept this great gap between rich and poor. There's less and less in between, less and less of a middle class. That shakes me up. I get very disturbed by what gets done to the environment in the name of business. You know, if you spend time in Europe, or you spend time in Canada, and then you come back to America, you see the omnipresence of violence and the way that we seem to accept the inevitability of that. That bothers me a lot. If you're asking me what do I do about it, I write to the degree that I can without masking what I understand the truth to be. I don't know that writers, as writers, can necessarily change things very much. Writers have to tell the truth from the angle that they see it. They can't hope necessarily to change society. What they can do is present society with a picture of itself and then, if that society chooses to change, then that's fine, but if I really wanted to mold behavior more than I'm doing, or to alter actions, I would be in politics. You know, a fair number of writers do have political ends, but I don't. Not in the way they do.

So why aren't you in politics? I'd have somebody to vote for.

Because like a lot of writers, I'm most comfortable sitting in a room, rather than standing in front of crowds.

Today, just today, you've been interviewed by three people, I believe, and have yet to do a reading. How are you surviving that?

Well, I was saying to somebody the other day that the one dimension to the writer's life that has come to surprise me is that I always thought it would be a solitary occupation. The way the book business is changing, it's now a much more public role. The author is expected to promote his or her own work, to appear on television, to be on the radio, to give interviews. I won't say that it's become part of showbiz, but there is an element of having to put yourself forward in the media that I would never have expected if you had told me thirty years ago when I was in my twenties what my life would be when I came to be fifty-three years old. I just wouldn't have thought it possible that writing a book would also involve the things that I am asked to do. It's a big change.

Would you have thought that you could have done those things?

No, because in those days I had a problem with shyness. I had great difficulties getting up in front of audiences. It's not unknown among writers. Over the years I've simply had to become accustomed to these things, these activities, because I'm asked to do them so often.

Well, thank you so very much. Is there anything that you thought I ought to have asked?

No, no, no, interviewers should ask what they want to ask.

But I did wonder something. Early on in *The Feast of Love*, Charlie is walking around and he comes up with a word that doesn't exist in our language: glimmerless. And I wondered if you were going to notice that.

I did indeed notice.

Paul Rawlins

My brothers chose this picture—
presumably for the look on my face.

Paul Rawlins works as an editor and writer in Salt Lake City, Utah. His fiction has appeared in *Sycamore Review, Prism International, Paris Transcontinental*, and other journals, and has received numerous awards, including the Flannery O'Connor Award for his first short-story collection, *No Lie Like Love* (University of Georgia Press).

PAUL RAWLINS

Ours

> ... I imagined
> for a long time that the baby, since
> it would have liked to smell our clothes to know
> what a mother and a father would have been,
> hovered sometimes in our closet ...

> —Robert Hass, "On Squaw Peak"

*T*he ghosts of children haunt our house. They gather at corners, huddle in the closet just above the mound of heavy winter clothes piled on the upper shelf. There's a coolness you sense when you draw on a sweater, the edge of a scent that scurries up and past you, a column of clean, bright air instead of musty wool. I take this to mean that, whatever, whoever they really are, they want to be close—but so far as I know, they can't be touched.

In the backyard this spring, they've taken to hanging from the dripping limbs of the peach tree. Teddy, our dog, knows they're there. He'll whine to be let out the back door, then trot over to the tree, where he sits on his haunches and stares up into the branches. I followed him out once to check for nests or maybe stray leaves—frozen, black ones that had clung through the winter and might be making a shadow or a sound—but there was nothing. Teddy looked back at me over his dog shoulder to make sure I saw whatever it was, too, or to check that he was doing okay—he had that look of wanting to know he was doing this thing right. I nodded, and he went back to watching the tree while I stayed there looking past the branches to the marly sky until the water coming up from the grass had soaked through my shoes and I could feel the chill in my feet.

"Come on, Teddy," I said. He followed me to the patio, but when I slid the door open and stepped inside, he turned and jogged back to the tree. He came in later, scratching at the glass door after dark. Lystra, my wife, stared from the kitchen table while he hustled past her to the porch, where we heard him lapping from his dish. Lystra stacked my plate on top of hers without saying anything, then carried them to the sink.

She knows they're out there, too, and when Teddy came back through the kitchen, she crouched down to take his pointed face in her hands.

"You're a good dog, Teddy," she said, then let him go.

Lystra goes on with her housework, her gardening, the grocery business she runs over the phone, taking a bath, all of it with them around her. She surprised me the first time I went to tell her I'd felt as though there were someone perched on the arm of the couch. I thought maybe I'd seen something, too—a smudge, or a tear in what should have been seamless air—and the hair rose on the back of my neck. I found Lystra in our bedroom, folding towels and sheets. She stopped long enough to look up when I came in the room, then went back to pinching a pale green towel in the middle between her fingers, folding it in half again lengthwise, quickly, as though she were clapping her hands.

"I know," she said when I told her.

"You know what?" I asked. I scooted the laundry basket over and sat on the edge of the bed until she scowled at me. We'd just bought a new, fancy mattress, a thick one with white-on-white striped ticking that was stuffed with layers of horsehair and spun-cotton batting. We were supposed to turn and rotate it head to foot every first of the month, and we weren't supposed to sit on the edge—no jumping, either, of course.

I pulled a chair over.

"You know what?" I asked her again. It was only a weird feeling I had come to tell her about, really.

"They come and go," she said while she bussed a stack of folded towels to the hall linen closet.

"Who?"

"Those children," she told me from the doorway, where she stood with her arms folded across her stomach. She had just cut her hair short, the way women do sometimes in their thirties, and it had left her face looking more open, fuller. "They're children," she said again. Then she came for her wicker laundry basket on the bed and left for the washroom downstairs.

I know that Lystra's tried ignoring them. I have, too, but you can't always or forever. She's tried to guess what they might want, but there's nothing she can think of to do for them. She can't feed them and doesn't believe they could be cold, only lonesome, perhaps. I have heard her sing songs while she works around the house, silly ones that children want, with nonsense rhymes like "hey diddly, diddly, dye-die-die" and such. She sings under her breath, almost to herself, in that unconscious way you do when you're thinking about something which makes you sing, rather than the song itself.

She never used to sing. It used to be the radio when we first married, eleven years ago, and she couldn't stand the quiet of the house when I was working swing shift and she was home for hours alone before me. I came home one day, and she had bought a little black Sony with luminous green numbers that from then on she left playing on the kitchen counter.

She got used to being home alone when she started her grocery business. The radio stayed on, but it stayed turned down to where it was forgotten, and we sometimes heard it from our bed at night. That led to a game we used to play after one of us got up to go turn it off, where the one left behind might or might not hide in the dark house along the way back to the bedroom. It was terrifying to walk back, and then, if you survived, to find the bedclothes rumpled and empty. You had to look for the other one if they were gone— that was the rule—and no lights. When it was me, searching for Lystra, I used to close my eyes sometimes, squatting on my haunches and swirling my hands out in front of me. Somehow this seemed to put us on more even footing. Sometimes I would feel her heat as she moved past my reach, a fold in the air at my side, luring me down the hall. Once she even hurdled over my shoulder, brushing me like a bat might, or an owl swooping past in the doorway of a barn when your eyes hadn't yet adjusted to the dark.

That game is an old one. Lystra stays up now on her own, while I go to bed myself. I'll wake up after an hour or two most nights to see if she's there. Sometimes she'll answer from the bathroom or the patio; a light will switch off, and then she'll lift the covers and slide into bed. Other times I find her in the kitchen with her glasses on, reading at the table. Or in the spare bedroom, sitting with her feet up on the daybed, the curtains opened to let in light from outdoors that turns her nightgown pale and silver.

"Usually they're pretty quiet," is what she told me when I asked if something in the house was keeping her up. "They go to bed at night, I guess, like everybody else."

I can't think of spirits needing sleep—spirits, clouds, reflections, dust, whatever I've thought them to be once.

"They're only children," my wife reminds me. "They've got to have their rest."

They're our children, of course. By my wife's count, there could be at least five of them. There have been five she knows of. Two more she suspects. Others rejected by her body early—maybe in the first moments, maybe hours later, as if my seed is poison to her, or the eggs she bears are hollow, like the ones we've blown for Easter, thin and practically translucent, with no more strength than tissue.

We talked nonstop after we lost the first, trying to be sensitive to one another, to reassure ourselves. It was so common—how many friends did we have who had gone through it?—that it seemed it could have been our due, but now the odds were with us. Our lovemaking became fraught with determination to make a child so beautiful, so perfect and strong, as though our raucous force could assure it—as though we could pound nails a little deeper and set the seams and joints too tight to leak or split. As though strong love alone could produce strong life—which, perhaps, it has. But no bodies that could live in light and air.

The second was followed closely by a third. And then hiatus. Rest. An autumn season, and a winter, as things go, with the silences that grow up between you when a part of life is scarred beyond the point of your being able to keep looking at it.

The next time we were cautious. I curled around Lystra afterward, and she seemed to make herself small to fit, as though I were a shell or a case closing snug around a jewel. She finally stopped shaking and she went to sleep, while I kept watch for most the night and made my bargains there with God or whoever might be listening.

The next time was by accident. Since then, we've grown more careful.

Lystra started the grocery business she runs out of our home because this was where she planned to stay and raise her babies. She quit her job the week after she found out she was pregnant the first time, because she wanted to make her recruits and get her system pat long before the baby came. The business was going to save us money while it made us money, too, which it has. Lystra has seven women under her now in her downline, plus her best customers, whom she's on the phone with once a week taking orders. The commodities are bought in bulk, and Lystra arranges for drops and distribution from our garage. My wife and two out of the seven women under her have done well with this system, providing toothpaste and toilet paper, cold cereals, diapers, canned goods, even an off-brand motor oil and tires for their neighbors.

She keeps the business up, she says, because she likes it. I worried that it would remind her of why she started it in the first place, of all the plans we'd hatched while she lay there patient as I thumped her naked belly, claiming that I was testing it for ripeness, pretending I knew anything at all about what was going on inside of her.

The grocery business doesn't have anything to do with that anymore, she tells me, and the women she sells goods to are her friends. Her business now isn't supposed to be any different than the home we live in, which has three bedrooms with room for more and sits in a neighborhood where herds of elementary-aged children walk past to school in the mornings and scream through the streets in the summers. Downstairs there is still masking tape on the floors from two more bedrooms we had planned, and a long family room we argued over whenever it came up—over how big it needed to be, colors, a fireplace, carpet, lights. We marked the rooms off with the tape, sticking it down, then measuring and pulling it up again, over and over, to move the imaginary walls. It's all just grey space down there now, and junk, aside from a laundry room.

Lystra said once that these children don't go down there, and it's true, I've never noticed them to. They stay upstairs, where we are mostly, and I've seen Lystra haul the ironing board up to the living room or kitchen for no other reason I know. Even so, they never do come around directly—and they don't stay if you move toward them.

I was arguing once with Lystra about it, not sure what was going on. I wanted to know, if these things were really there, what they were hiding all the time for, whether they were teasing us or if they were afraid.

"I don't know," Lystra said. "They might just be upset about what's going on."

"So you think whatever they are, they're mad at us?"

"They could be angry, but not necessarily at us. You see what I mean?" Lystra said. "Angry that this happened, but not because it's our fault."

"It's not our fault," I said.

"I know it," Lystra said.

It's something I've told and retold her, and sometimes she's told me, around the table, in our bed, digging in the flowers out in the backyard. You take turns at being the one who knows, like you take turns at being most everything after you've been together for awhile—the strong one, the grouch, coach, prophet, martyr.

Flowers are something new to Lystra and me, a hobby she took up on her own a few years back. There's no history of it in her family or mine, but I've gotten to where I like joining her to work on the egg-shaped hills we've mounded up in the front yard and in back. There's a familiarity to it now I enjoy, the triangular holes cut by the little hand shovels, the transplants from the nursery with their cubes of soft new roots cupped in my palm, Lystra's yellow watering can with a grinning frog on the side.

This year, Lystra wanted the sweet alyssum she planted in the backyard last season taken out. Out back she wanted tulips now, and in front, roses. It was cool out, overcast and damp, but we were working anyway, wearing windbreakers and kneeling on burlap sacks to keep dry and out of the mud. Off as the day was, it was still the warmest yet all year. While we were digging, there might have been something on the step. They stayed, mostly, at the edge of things, and you saw more when you weren't trying.

This year, Lystra wanted a scarecrow for the garden, too. She had an old coat and a pair of denim coveralls wadded up in a box in the garage, and I'd noticed she'd been adding other items—a hat, which seemed obvious, and a bandanna, a pair of threadbare gardening gloves to make hands, a pillowcase she'd embroidered with a face. I'd seen last week that we were going to have a smiling scarecrow, friendly and benign—one who would probably go ahead and husk the corn for the birds. It would be a scarecrow these children would like, like one of the old men at church who passed candy from his pockets to the kids when they shook hands.

When something moved around the corner of the house, I stabbed my shovel into the soil and sat back on my sack, looking at the peach tree with Teddy under it, wagging. I had thrown a rock at that tree just last fall, sent it cracking up through the branches so that it startled Teddy and landed somewhere in the neighbor's yard. I made Teddy come inside, and he spent the afternoon whining at the door until I shut him in the garage. I don't know if it was Teddy or the rock I was feeling guilty for, but I'd gone back out later that night while Lystra was in the shower and stood there in front of the tree feeling foolish.

"We've tried," is what I finally said. "We wanted you. If you're really here, you know that." A neighbor had a sprinkler running, a rain bird, and there were crickets chirruping, but nobody answered. I checked behind me to see that the bathroom light was still on in the house before I went on. "You should just go." I had my hands out, like I was holding a bowl, explaining, trying to win my case.

Now I sat with my hands wrapped around my knees while I stared across the yard. Behind me I heard Lystra stop jabbing at the earth while she rearranged her sack. The clouds were settling down the face of the mountains across the valley, grey and full of awful silence, driving everything indoors.

"What?" I said when I realized Lystra had been talking.

"Are you finished?"

"No," I said.

She waited, but I left my spade where it was and sat looking out over the yard until she said why didn't I go get a rake and start over at the corner.

In the garage I left the rake and drug out Lystra's scarecrow box and some old, dusty sacking with a coarse weave that burned my hands when I stuffed it down the pant legs I'd tied off at the ankles with twine. I used a coat hanger to help form shoulders and crammed the shirt sleeves with newspaper I knew was only going to deteriorate from the wet. For the torso, I pulled two pillows off the bed. I shoved one halfway down into the tops of the pants, then folded the shirt around the other and tucked it behind the bib of the overalls. For the head, I used a dirty foam basketball. I snugged Lystra's pillow slip around it, tied it off at the neck, then stared at the grinning face before I turned it around backwards. I practiced faces on the floor of the garage with a piece of charcoal. I drew a smile and then a frown. Then I worked on a scowl, something that looked like a scream, then a snarl with jagged saw teeth. Finally, I settled on a howl—three elongated Os, two for the eyes and a long, distended mouth.

I found a hammer, and I hauled the straw man outside, flapping limp under my arm.

Lystra was back on her haunches, watching as I came out of the garage.

"Where are you going to put it?" she said. She got up to help, brushing off her knees, but I turned up the back steps instead of heading for the garden.

"What are you doing?" Lystra said.

I let the scarecrow slump on the porch so I could drive a nail an inch deep into the back door, then I hung him there, looking out at the tree where Teddy stood with his nose turned up toward the empty branches. Lystra moved back to the edge of the patio to look. She stood with her hands on her hips, then motioned me out of the way. I went down the steps and stood halfway between her and the door until she started to laugh.

"Was it supposed to be scary?" she said.

"I guess so."

She nodded; then she turned sober.

"He looks more like somebody kicked him in the balls."

I turned back and saw the face, eyes and mouth wide in shock and innocence, with less menace than there was fear. I squatted, banging at the grass with the hammer.

"Are you going to leave him there?" Lystra said.

"Are they still waiting, is that it?" I said. "Is there still supposed to be a chance?"

Lystra shook her head.

"This isn't limbo or purgatory or whatever. Why should they have to stay here?"

"I don't know," Lystra said. She tossed her silver garden claw toward the flower bed and squeezed her hands between her knees. "Unless they're just ours."

I felt a raindrop splash on the back of my hand.

"How can they be ours? How can they be anything?" I said.

"That's just what they are," Lystra said.

"That's crazy."

"If that's what you want to be." Lystra sounded stern.

I stood and looked out over the yard. "Teddy," I yelled. "Get over here." While he jogged over I turned back to

Lystra. "What would you do if I cut that tree down right now? It's old, and the fruit's never any good. I think it's got peach bore."

"Do what you want," Lystra said. She was trying to keep her eyes on me and away from the spot where Teddy had been standing.

"You don't think I could. You watch."

"You could," Lystra said. She bent down for her gloves where she'd dropped them. "I know you could. What good's it going to do?"

When she got to the top of the steps, she lifted the straw man off his nail. She twisted his head around, turned the smiling face out and looked at it for a minute; then she pushed him over the porch rail into the flowers and went inside.

The exhaustion that came with living in our house surfaced sometimes and burst over everything in an enervating flood, and I found Lystra on the bed, asleep, when I went in. It was after I'd thrown the hammer out in the yard and sworn at Teddy, then locked him in his pen when he wouldn't stay away from the tree. I'd gathered up the garden tools, stacked the sacks of bulbs and peat moss in the garage. The scarecrow I sat up in a plastic chair under the eaves, safe from the rain, his grinning face turned out to the world in welcome.

To watch Lystra while she slept, you wouldn't know she wasn't perfect. But there was something inside of us that couldn't come out and wouldn't be kept in. Something inside of us that made shades instead of children. We weren't supposed to try anymore. There were reasons, one on top of the other, all things the doctors understood. And there had been doctors, one after another, for Lystra and for me. Doctors with no shame, for whom your most private moments, your starkest nakedness meant nothing. We'd had arguments as well as silence, fights vicious enough to leave bruises inside that you couldn't see a way to keep from rising to your skin. And at different times we practiced hope, or we tried for understanding.

"You're going to adopt," my mother told Lystra after the last time, after we had considered this and everything else. She had said it before. "You're going to raise a wonderful family, and they'll be yours, one hundred percent yours." It was what we probably would do, we'd decided. We just didn't know when. We were always thinking it would be soon. I didn't know, though, and Lystra didn't know if we could ever crowd these others out. They might be jealous or cause trouble—or, then, they might just leave. You couldn't say.

I rested my chin on Lystra's shoulder while I lay beside her, wanting to tell her that, to tell her anything just to hear us talk. The mattress we'd bought raised the bed four inches, and from the dripping window I could see Teddy out back. I'd let him out of his run, and when the storm had started, he'd come in from the yard to lie in the doorway of his doghouse. That's where he was now, with his long face cradled between his paws, looking out to where the tree stood beading up with rain, keeping watch over everything that love had made.

Sergio Gabriel Waisman

Buenos Aires, 1972.

Sergio Gabriel Waisman is a writer and translator, born in the United States to Argentine parents. He received an MA in creative writing from the University of Colorado, Boulder, and is completing his PhD in the Department of Spanish and Portuguese at the University of California, Berkeley. His translation of Ricardo Piglia's *Assumed Name* received the Meritorious Achievement Award in the 1995 Eugene M. Kayden National Translation Contest. His most recent translation is *Juan de la Rosa*, by Nataniel Aguirre (Oxford University Press, 1998). His own fiction and poetry have appeared in *Hanging Loose, TAMAQUA, ACM (Another Chicago Magazine), Santa Clara Review*, and others. He is currently working on a novel entitled *Leaving*.

SERGIO GABRIEL WAISMAN
The Watchmaker's Son

*J*he watchmaker is not in today; his son is covering the shop for him, although he knows almost nothing about his father's trade. It has always been a mystery to him, the shop and the work, his father's job and what his days are like. His father always left home before his children finished having breakfast, kissed his two boys on top of their heads, lifted his two girls and hugged them in the air. I'm going to the shop, I have timepieces to fix, is what his family heard him say every morning while they were still half-asleep, and off he would go for the entire day, not come back until after 10 P.M. on most days, after they had already had dinner, and even later on others. And then there were the arguments between the father and the mother, she screaming at him when he left, greeting him with more screams when he returned at night. And the two sons, always fighting when they should be getting ready for school, while the oldest daughter played with the young- est, a baby girl, as if she were the mother.

But today was different. You're coming with me, he had said to him during breakfast, you can go to the afternoon session of school straight from the shop. His mother had argued, the usual phrases and raised voices, plus the theft of one of her children on this day, but to no avail. After they had made it out of the family fray, father and son walked together in complete silence, the serious mood of the city streets at that time of morning reflected on the father's face, and in turn imitated by the son, for exactly four long blocks down Avenida Warnes, then left on Malabia for three shorter ones further, at which point they stopped at a corner, one block before Avenida Corrientes. The boy had been to his father's shop only once before, and that long ago, when he was much younger. This time, he did not see it at first, and could not even tell there was a storefront where they were standing. The entrance was a small door nearly hidden against the wall of a tall building. You're covering the shop this morning, son. I'll check back periodically. If anyone comes for a pickup, just tell them I'll be back in the afternoon. If they want to leave something, fill out one of these. He showed him the order forms, and the tags to attach to each piece to be repaired. Whatever you do, don't give anyone anything, and don't leave the shop, okay? There shouldn't be too many customers anyway. Most of them come after lunch. I'll be back soon.

Now the watchmaker's son—the eleven year old who has never been on vacation, has never been outside Buenos Aires, not even to the Tigre Delta; who has spent the majority of his life in the vicinity of his neighborhood, between Chacarita and Villa Crespo—stands inside the shop that is more a kiosk stuck into a wall than an actual store. His first time there since that initial visit, five or six years ago, he could not remember exactly, when he had been brought there with his brother and sisters by their mother to see their father's new shop. Smaller than he remembered, it is even more spectacular in a sense, for no space is wasted—the tight room is filled with old clocks hanging on every centimeter of wall space, mechanisms and various parts and tools piled everywhere in boxes opened and closed (the boy does not know their names, but is sure that if his father were there he could tell him what each one was called), and a crowded workbench beyond which is the window looking out at the street.

He stands next to the tall stool, does not dare to climb up and sit on it yet. His father's high stool and workbench. The stool comes up to his chest, the workbench nearly above his head—the watchmaker's son is short and heavy—and he feels dwarfed inside the shop even though his father must feel like a giant in there. It is a strange, magical place, with all the clocks on the walls stopped at different hours and none of them working, as if time had ceased to run in a thousand different imaginary countries, in different time zones, at a different time in each. And the radio, mounted on the wall opposite the window, the source of the old tangos his father sings to himself when he is home, as if he were still there in the shop, working and listening and singing along, always a raspy longing in his low voice.

The watchmaker's son does not want to sit down. He would rather stand there and imagine his father sitting on the high stool, legs bent under him and resting on the bar, large upper body stooped over the workbench, a white rectangle of light coming in through the window facing the street, concentrating with his grey-green eyes, broad eyebrows, and thick set of hair, holding a silver pocket watch in his left hand and a thin screwdriver in his right (the watchmaker's son is sure that it must have a special name, this fine-tipped screwdriver, and the other tools his father uses, only he doesn't know them). He imagines his father performing an operation on the graceful instrument of time that is as precise as surgery. He can almost hear his father singing along to the music from the radio now, like he does in the morning before he leaves for work, when everyone else is still getting up, humming under his breath (*Soy hijo de Buenos Aires, por apodo 'El Porteñito,' el criollo más compadrito, que en esta tierra nació*) as he manipulates the mechanism under the face of the timepiece (What is that screwdriver called—if he only knew!), the tiny wheels and gears usually out of sight revealed to his father like a patient's insides to a surgeon.

A man cannot function in this society without a good watch, his father always says; it is as important as having a strong heart and a bit of luck on your side. Every kitchen should have a clock on its wall, everyone needs an alarm clock next to his bed, and every man should have a watch in his chest pocket. Repairing clocks is like keeping time going. The whole country—the whole world—would come to a screeching halt if there were no watchmakers like me, it would be like a man without his own heart! The youth imagines his father thinking this as he adjusts a minute screw with that tool (What could its name be, good God?!), then closes the face back over the naked mechanisms, winds the gear, and looks on as the second hand starts to tick on the face of the watch inside the silver casing.

He looks up, past the workbench and through the small window into the street, observes the people hurrying down Malabia toward the corner of Corrientes, where the entrance to the subway is. Line B, from Federico Lacroze all the way downtown and on to the port at Leandro N. Alem, the boy says to himself. It must be eighty-five meters from his father's shop (the watchmaker's son likes to estimate distances like this, to be able to measure the world and oneself in it in concrete terms). The people are well dressed, mostly men in dark suits and jackets, ties, leather shoes and briefcases, and some women in secretary skirts and stockings, their hair pulled back or tied up, heels shaping the curve of their ankles and calves. Looking out, the boy wonders how many of those men have pocket watches; all the fancier-dressed ones do, he is sure. They would not be going about their day so seriously, he says to himself, if they did not have time tucked inside their suit pockets; they would lose track of everything, they would constantly have to stop and ask somebody what time it was, losing precious seconds and minutes in the process. And the ladies wear their slender wristwatches, almost like bracelets (women's wrists and ankles so much more delicate than men's)—although he did not see too many of these in his father's shop, he was not sure why; still he was certain the women, too, would bring their watches there if they broke down. They could not afford to be without a watch either, especially if they worked outside the home—unlike his mother, who was always home when he left in the morning, when he came back for lunch, when he came home after school. His father's shop was so perfectly located, right in front of all those people, where they could drop off their watches if they broke down, get them fixed before they lost too much time without them. As I have always thought, the watchmaker's son thinks, you have to have a timepiece not just to know what time it is, but to actually *have* time. Without a watch or a clock, you are lost, timeless, wandering aimlessly without direction. You are stuck in a past that no longer exists without any chance of recovering your present and your future.

The eleven year old turns back to the tall stool, decides he is going to try to sit on it. If he is going to be there—to occupy the space his father usually occupies, even if it is only temporarily, for a couple of hours or so while he takes care of some business around the corner, as his father said before leaving him there all alone—then he might as well do it in style. Act like he imagines his father would (without breaking anything, of course). So he reaches up to the wall behind him and turns on the radio. Already tuned to the right station, a tango blares out mid-song from among all the different frozen times on the wall next to it. Then he turns back around and begins the climb onto his father's chair. He thinks it is going to be difficult, him being only a boy still, really (but into the second decade of his life, he likes to tell himself), and a bit on the heavy side at that (so much more like his mother physically than like his father, but at least he has his father's eyes and hair, he thinks to himself). He manages to jump right up, however (I must be getting more agile, he thinks), and before he knows it he is sitting on the tall stool, his legs under him, his elbows on the large workbench, the rectangle of light from the window right in front of him, the music filling the shop from behind him. (*No hay ninguno que me iguale, para enamorar mujeres, puro hablar de pareceres, puro filo y nada más.*) The tango comes in scratched, the song sounding not as if it came from a meter behind him (the distance the boy estimates), but rather from far away—or from one of the many times on the broken clocks hanging on the wall, he thinks.

He looks out the window at the street from a different perspective now, sitting on the tall stool, higher up, more clear. This is how my father must see things, he says to himself, and tries to hum along to the song, not because he knows the tune, but because he is certain that that is what his father would be doing. Then he reaches down, grabs an old pocket watch from a box under the table, with the casing broken off and only one hand left. From the tool set on the table he takes a very thin, delicate screwdriver (it is the one he was wondering about before, only now he does not care so much what its name might be), and acts as if he is about to fix the watch. Just like my father, he says to himself, staring at the broken timepiece in his fat little hand, and begins to cry.

Ann Pancake

*Me and Daisy in 1966 on the
front porch of my grandparents' house.*

Ann Pancake's short-story collection, *Given Ground*, won the 2000 Bakeless Prize and will be published by the University of New England this summer. She has been the recipient of an NEA grant, and her short stories have appeared in a number of magazines, including the *Virginia Quarterly*, *Shenandoah*, and *Massachusetts Review*. She teaches creative writing and literature at Penn State Erie.

ANN PANCAKE
Redneck Boys

ichard has gone on and died, she thinks when
she hears the knuckle on the door. Took two weeks after the
accident, he was strong. The other three dead at the scene. She
reaches for the pack of cigarettes between Richard's New
Testament and the digital clock. The yellow stink of the
hospital still hangs in her hair. It's 3:07 A.M., and Richard has
gone on and died.

She pulls on yesterday's jeans and feels her way through the
hall, not ready yet for a light in her eyes. Cusses when she hits
barefoot the matchbox cars her son's left lying around. She's
so certain it's her brother, who was made messenger back
towards the beginning of this mess, she doesn't even pull back
the curtain to see. She stops behind the door to steady her
breath, which is coming quick and thin even though she's
expected the news for days. But when she unbolts the door, it
is a boy, a man, she hasn't seen in a few years.

He blows steam in the porchlight, straddling the floor frame
Richard never had time to finish. Coatless, his arms pork-
colored in the cold. He has forced himself into corduroy pants
he's outgrown and wears a pair of workboots so mudcaked
they've doubled in size. He grins. She knew him some time
ago. And he grins at her, his face gone swollen, then loose

under the chin, the way boys get around here.

"Cam," is what he says.

She draws back to let Splint pass. He unlaces the muddy boots and leaves them on the ground under the porch frame. The surprise she may have felt if he'd shown up before Richard's wreck—and she's not sure she would have felt surprise then—has been wrung out of her by the two-week vigil. Splint walks to the sofa where he wraps himself in an afghan and chafes his upper arms with his palms. He swipes at the runny nose with his shoulder. Cam remembers what she's wearing—just a long-john shirt of Richard's over the jeans, no bra—and for a moment, her face heats with self-consciousness. Then the heat leaves her face for other places in her body. Angry at herself, Cam wills the heat away.

"Where's your boy?" Splint asks. Then, "I heard about Richard."

"Down to Mom's," Cam answers.

"You're up on this mountain without even a dog at night?"

Splint squats in front of the woodstove, still shawled in the afghan that doesn't quite fall to his waist. Cam watches the soft lobs between the waistband of the corduroys and the hem of the hiked-up T-shirt. Burrs snagged in his pantscuffs. Cam wonders what he's done now to end up coatless in the middle of a freezing night. Then she doesn't wonder. She crouches on the edge of the sofa behind him, her chest clenched, and she waits for what he'll do next.

What he does is open the stove door and huddle up to it closer, giving Cam a better look at his soft back. Hound-built he was as a boy, a little bowlegged and warped along the spine, the new muscles riding long and taut and rangy right under the skin. Freckle-ticked shoulders. She recalls trailing him one August afternoon up a creekbed where he'd stashed a six-pack of Old Milwaukee in sycamore roots. He'd outgrown that shirt, too, a tank top, and she had watched it ride up, watched the tight small of his back. The muscles coming so soon, too early, on those boys.

"Why don't you poke up the fire for me?" Splint startles her. She starts to move, then pauses, asks herself who she's answering to and why. But she's been raised to obedience. She leans forward and picks up a split chunk on the hearth. Its raw insides tear the skin on her palm, even though it is a hard hand that has handled many stove logs. She shoves the log in the embers, kneels, and blows until the coals flare up. Then, as she reaches to shut the door, Splint's own hand snakes out of the afghan and grabs her arm. Cam goes icy in the roots of her hair. She yanks away, harder than she needs to. The stove door stays open, the pipe drawing hard and loud. A sizzle and whupping in the flue.

"It's too bad about Richard," Splint says. "He was always a good boy."

Cam can't tell if he's mocking her.

"And a hard worker, huh?"

This is funeral talk, and Cam doesn't answer.

"You never were a big talker," Splint says. "Guess you don't got any cigarettes around here?"

He pulls a big splinter from the stove to light the Virginia Slim she gives him. Cam knows he knows Richard is just like the others. Went down off the mountain at five A.M. to meet his ride, traveled two hours to build northern Virginia condominiums all day, traveled the hundred miles back to a six-room house he was putting together on weekends and didn't finish before the wreck. Celotex walls and the floors unsanded. Yeah, Richard was a hard worker, just like all the other boys. Only Splint wouldn't work hard, and Splint ended up in jail.

"I still think about you," he says. He'd been staring into the stove, but now he cocks his head sideways to look at Cam, kneeling a little behind him. She has her bare feet drawn up under her, and not just for warmth. To be all of a piece like that, pulled together, makes her feel safe from herself. Her eyes drift to his hands in the firelight there, them hanging loose in his lap. It occurs to her she has never seen them so clean, although the heat draws an odor from his body, the odor of ground in the woods. But the hands—no grease in the knuckle creases or in the prints, the nails clear and unbroken. Back when she knew him, the hands were all the time dirty. He spent half his time with his head in an engine, the other half under the chassis. Frittered his cash away on parts and auto-wrecker junk, and when it still wouldn't run, he'd steal. What've you been into now, buddy? Cam thinks. Splint pulls up the tail of his shirt to stop his running nose.

The second time she and Splint ran, they were thirteen. They met at the end of her road right around dawn, the hills smoking fog twists and a damp raw in the air. They flagged the Greyhound when it came, the Greyhound would pick you up anywhere back then, but although they'd had their sights set on North Carolina, the money Splint thieved off his older sister got them no farther than middle-of-nowhere Gormania. When the driver realized they'd ridden past how far they could pay, he threw them off at a mountaintop truck stop and told the cook to call the sheriff.

The deputy who showed up had only one ear. He phoned their parents with the receiver flat against the earhole. It was Cam gave him the numbers, and Splint wouldn't speak to her for four weeks after. She remembers Splint all tough over his black coffee in that drafty restaurant, pretending Cam wasn't there. The waitress locking up the cigarette machine. The deputy told her how his ear got shot off stalking deer poachers, but after he left, the cook said his wife did it with sewing scissors. When Splint's dad appeared, three hours later, he, too, pretended Cam wasn't there. He jerked Splint to his feet and dragged him out behind the building while Cam slunk along the wall to watch. Splint slouched between the Stroehmann bread racks and raw kitchen slop. The scraggly garbage birds in a panic. But his father just looked at him and shook his head, then cussed him without imagination. The same two words, over and over, his voice flat as an idling motor. In the constant wind across the mountaintop, his father's coveralls flapped against his legs, making them look skinnier than they were. Finally he threw a milk crate at Splint. Splint caught it.

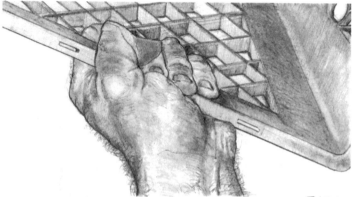

"Oh, you were bright," Splint is saying, and she winces at how the gravel has come in his craw. Tobacco voice. "Bright. All that running around you did and they still gave you a scholarship."

Cam doesn't answer back. Splint knows there was one person in their class as bright as Cam, and that was Splint. He knows what she got instead of a college degree. She realizes she's unnumbed enough to need a drink, and she heads to the kitchen to fetch one. Aware of what Splint will want, she starts to open the refrigerator, then stops. On the door, her boy's drawings, motorcycles, and eighteen-wheelers. Instead, she pulls a bottle of Jim Beam and two jelly glasses from the crates they are using until they have money for cabinets. The whiskey she and Richard shared, but the beer in the refrigerator belongs to just Richard.

She even called Splint once or twice during the year she spent at the university in grey Morgantown. Then she left the state and saw a little of the world, ha. Waited tables in Daytona for eight months before she met a boy named Eric, and they went west; that was for six. What she remembers best—or worst—at any rate, what she remembers clearest—is the way this Eric talked. In six months, she never could get used to it. Hardened every consonant, choked up every vowel. Such an awkward, a cramped way to work your words out of your mouth. It got to where she couldn't stand to hear him say her name, how he'd clip it off, one syllable. Cam. Like he had no idea about the all of her. Back home, they speak it full. They say it Ca-yum. Back here.

Splint drains his glass, shivers his head and shoulders, stretches. The afghan drops to the floor. He swaggers over to Richard's gun cabinet, and Cam sees how he carries himself like a middle-aged man. Still small in his hips, he is, but big across the belly, and him no more than thirty. Although her eyes stay on Splint, her mind sees her own body at the same time. She knows she's gone in the other direction, a rare way to go around here. Cam knows she's worn rutted and flat. Splint strokes the rifle stocks along their grains, draws one out and pretends to sight it down the hall. It is Richard's, and Cam feels an urge to lift it from Splint's hands. Between his third and fourth fingers, the cigarette smolders, there under the finger playing the trigger. "Pow," Splint says.

She'd known she'd never stay with Eric, but Richard was just something that happened when she came home for Christmas. Fifteen minutes in Richard's dad's pickup behind the Moose, the windows fogged, and then Richard sat up with his jeans around his ankles and printed their names in the steam. Like a twelve-year-old girl, Cam thought at the time. Some little twelve-year-old girl. No, she never felt for Richard what she felt for Splint. She was so fresh back home she was still homesick and she just wanted to hear them talk, talk to her; it could have been any boy who talked that way. She ran into Richard that night. But Richard was a good boy and a hard worker, everybody said so. She could have done way worse; her mom made sure to remind her of this often. After a while, she wrote Eric in Phoenix. (Seventy-five, eighty miles an hour across that flat Oklahoma, Texas, New Mexico. Highways like grooves, and the land. She fixed that land, she remade it every night. She dreamed it green where it was brown, rumpled it where flat.) He wrote back once. Told her he always knew she'd end up with some redneck boy.

The last time she and Splint ran, they were seniors in high school. Splint told her to meet him a ways down her road so her parents wouldn't see, and he showed up in a brand-new Camaro; she recognized the car. Sixteenth-birthday present to some lawyer's kid at school, but Splint was playing his own music. Lynyrd Skynyrd. Cam got drunk before they hit the paved road, grain alcohol and orange pop, the music thrushing through her stomach and legs, while Splint cussed the car for handling like a piece of shit. She cranked down her window, stuck her head in the wind. Wind, leaves, hills, but no sky. Sky too far overhead to see from a car. Just ground, pounding by on either side. It was spring, and by that time, they knew about the college, the scholarship.

They eventually reached Frawl's Flat, the second straightest piece of road in the county, and they started seeing how fast the Camaro would go. Stupid-drunk like they were, the state police snuck up on them easy. Splint squealed off down the highway, and even though the car was a piece of shit, they might have outrun the cops, or, more likely, could have ditched the car and both run off in the woods. But Splint did something else.

He swerved back a narrow, heavy-wooded road, braked, and screamed at Cam to get out, shoving at her shoulder as he yelled. And Cam did. She tumbled out, the car down to maybe fifteen miles an hour by then, landed on her hip in the ditch, then scrambled up the shale bank into the scrub oak and sumac. The staties were so close they caught Splint where she could watch. Crouched in the brush, cold sober, she saw the three of them moving in and out of the headlights and taillights. He'd just turned eighteen, and they put him in jail for a while that time. They didn't know to look for Cam.

"I still think about you," Splint is saying again. He has put away the rifle and settles on the sofa, leaving her room which she doesn't take. He's trying to start something, but this time, she tells herself, she won't follow.

Richard always called it love. Ten years of late suppers and, even on weekends, him asleep in front of the TV by 8 P.M. Two hours later, he'd wake and they'd shift to the bed, the brief bucking there. Afterwards, he'd sleep again, as sudden and as deep as if he'd been cold-cocked. Richard was a good boy and a hard worker. And now he's waited for two weeks, in his patient, plodding way, to be killed in a car wreck. That week's driver asleep at the wheel ten miles short of home after a day of drywalling.

Cam feels as tired as if she'd been awake for all her thirty years.

The first time she and Splint had run, they were twelve years old, at 4-H camp. The camp lay five miles back a dirt road where they hauled kids in schoolbuses until the mountains opened into a sudden clearing along the river. Like a secret place. The county had turned 1950's chicken coops into bunkhouses and jammed them mattress to mattress with cast-off iron beds, and Cam slept uneasy there under the screenless windows, the barnboard flaps propped open for the little air.

She had seen Splint at school, but this was the first time she noticed. And as she watched from a distance, she heard what was live in him like a dog might hear it. What was live in him, she heard a high-pitched whine. The beds in the coop were packed so close together she could feel on her cheeks the night breath of the girls on either side. And the whine a hot line from her almost-breasts to her navel.

On the last evening, they had a Sadie Hawkins shotgun wedding, where the girls were supposed to catch the boys. The counselors lined them up, the boys with a fifty-foot headstart, then blew a whistle and turned them loose. Cam aimed at Splint. Splint knew she was after him, and he headed towards the river, where they were forbidden to go. All around Cam, big girls seized little squealy boys, older boys faked halfhearted escapes. Splint fled, but at twelve, Cam was his size, and as fast, and as strong. She saw him disappear in the treeline along the river, then she was dodging through trees herself, and she caught up with him on the rock bar there. Panting, but not yet spent, she reached out to grab him, but she got scared, then just touched at him like playing tag. Splint was trotting backwards, bent in at the waist, dodging and laughing. They heard others following them to the river, heard them hollering through the trees. "Pretend you ain't caught me yet," Splint said.

He wheeled and sloshed into the river, high stepping until the water hit his hips, then he dropped on his stomach and struck out swimming, Cam, just as strong, as swift, right behind.

The far side had no shore to it, just an eroded mud bank. They hauled themselves up the exposed maple roots, and then they were in woods, they were hidden, alone. Cam was twelve years old; she thought she knew what to do. Splint grappled her back, too much teeth in the kiss, his hands in unlikely places. They rubbed at each other through their soaked clothes, serious and quick, and the threat of the others swimming the river pushed them faster.

Cam was finding her way, so absorbed it was like being asleep, when she realized Splint wasn't doing anything back. He rolled away from her into the weeds and sat up with his face between his knees, his thin back to her. Too naive to feel hurt, Cam crawled closer. She heard a strange little animal noise that made her want to pet. Finally, she understood Splint was crying.

Something taps her feet folded under her. Splint has rolled his jelly glass across the floor.

"Girl, if you don't talk to me, I'm going to do something drastic."

Cam looks at him. "What are you doing up here in the middle of the night without a coat?"

Splint laughs, soft. "Got into it with a girl driving home. She threw me out of her car." He rises off the sofa, leans down to open the stove door, and strips away his T-shirt. He stands fat in front of the fire, soaking heat into his skin.

Cam's all the time finding her own boy sketching pickup trucks and stock cars on notebook paper. Oh, he is careful, detailed and neat. Until the very end. Then something breaks in him, unstops, and he turns violent and free. He gouges deep black lines behind the vehicles to show how fast they can go. When he was littler, and they still lived in Richard's parents' basement, he'd ride the back of the couch like a motorcycle, forcing air through his lips for the throttle. That he is not Richard's, she is almost sure, but he seems not Eric's either. Seems mothered and fathered by her and the place. She stands next to Splint now, following his stare in the fire. Without looking at her, Splint lifts her hand and presses it against his naked side.

"I'm not having sex with you," Cam says.

"That's not how come I'm here," says Splint.

He drops her hand and walks to the closet behind the front door. He pulls out a quilted flannel shirt of Richard's and buttons it on. Shoving aside the blaze-orange hunting jacket and coats that belong to Cam, he finally reaches the end of the rack and mutters.

"He's got his good one back in the bedroom," Cam says.

She finds the big Sunday coat. Splint takes it. Cam doesn't think about offering him a ride until after he's gone.

He got mad about the crying, screwed his fists in his eyes and muddied his face. Cam mumbled it didn't matter. By that time, counselors were yelling at them from across the water, how much trouble they were in if they didn't come right back. Cam stood up and Splint followed. They crept out of the trees and climbed down the bank without looking at the grownups. They waded out to thigh-deep and started paddling.

They pulled that water slow, kicked sloppy. They were putting off their punishment. Cam remembers the water still springtime cold a foot under the surface—this was June. The eyeball-green of the river, and how you could see current only in the little bubble clusters gliding down its top. She swam a little behind Splint, her head about parallel with his stomach, and when she remembers back, she understands how young he was. Twelve, same as her, yes, but a boy-twelve, and she thinks of her own son and feels sad and shameful for how she did Splint.

Because she was so close to him as they swam, and because she couldn't help but look at him, and because the way they glided along cut the water clean—no foam to speak of, no wave—Cam saw clearly what happened next.

She saw Splint break his stroke to reach out and toss aside a floating stick. His legs frogged behind him. This was about the solstice; it was still very light, she could see. He reached out, not looking too closely, not paying attention. He was just moving a thing in his way. But when Splint grabbed hold of the branch, Cam saw it liven in his fist and change shapes. She saw it spill water, jerk curvy in his hand. She saw it uncurl itself upright over Splint's head.

And was it a snake before he grabbed hold, or after he did? Cam used to wonder before she grew up. Now she only wonders why neither of them screamed.

*Siobhan Dowd of International PEN's Writers-in-Prison Committee in
London writes this column regularly, alerting readers to the plight of writers
around the world who deserve our awareness and our writing action.*

Silenced Voices:
U Pa Pa Lay and U Lu Zaw

by Siobhan Dowd

*O*f all countries where one might have been born in
recent times, Burma—or Myanmar as its illegitimate junta
redubbed it—might be the most dismal. Its citizens live in
abject poverty and fear; their daily lives are wracked with the
consequences of many years of corrupt rule. The place, despite great potential, lacks an effective infrastructure, with
health and social services which have been run into the
ground. The spread of such preventable diseases as AIDS is
rampant because of the military leadership's complete
disregard for human life. According to a United Nations in-

vestigator, the human-rights situation is deteriorating. The government brutally suppresses both opposition-party members and ethnic minorities. Choices are few for most Burmese citizens. For those who do have some resources, the sanest choice is probably to leave.

It is remarkable, then, that despite the hapless, hopeless nature of the place, troupes of comedians continue to travel the countryside, bringing with them a pithy mix of dance, drama, puppetry, and satire. The favorite topic of humor is the local daily news, and despite the dangers, the most commonly told jokes are about the government. These *Ah-nyeint* shows, as they are called, take place at all major celebrations: temple festivals, weddings, housewarmings, wakes, and anniversary parties. One of the most popular of all the troupes is the "Mustache Brothers," also known as "Myo Win Mar" ("Our Own Way"). Based in Mandalay, it was founded some thirty years ago by a now renowned family of acting talent. Among its most prominent members were the quartet Pa Pa Lay, aged fifty-three, his younger brothers Lu Ma and Ko Shwe Bo (the latter of whom made the puppets), and their cousin Lu Zaw, aged forty-nine. Between them, they comprised a Burmese version of the Marx Brothers. They were responsible for devising the shows, organizing tours, and writing and performing the comic sketches—that is, until five years ago, when U Pa Pa Lay and U Lu Zaw were arrested for a joke that was too blatant, and delivered in the wrong place at the wrong time.

Little is known about the Mustache Brothers' background and upbringing. The whole family, women included, have always participated in putting the shows together, whether in dance and choreography, devising costumes and make-up, or making puppets. The current generation was preceded by their fathers, who developed the style of putting the day-to-day tribulations of life into witty scenarios. The sketches used

up-to-the-minute local news, and were aimed at villagers and townspeople of all social classes. In 1991, U Pa Pa Lay was imprisoned for a year, merely for making a joke about the massive popularity of the National League for Democracy.

The National League for Democracy, or NLD, won a landslide victory in the general election of 1990. But to this day, the NLD's legitimate claim to rule has been denied by the military, which ignored the electorate's wishes by imprisoning the party's most prominent members. For many years it held its leader, the Nobel Laureate Daw Aung San Suu Kyi, under house arrest. Even today her movements are circumscribed, and there are regular roundups of NLD activists, many of whom languish in the country's infamous jails and labor camps. Understandably, most other comedians in Burma avoid showing obvious NLD sympathies; but the Mustache Brothers have always been visible in their support. Even after U Pa Pa Lay's first prison term, the troupe seemed uncowed. Their popularity perhaps afforded them some degree of protection, and no doubt care was taken that the jokes were funny without being too outspoken.

However, on January 4, 1996, the Mustache Brothers accepted an invitation they might have been wiser to refuse: they agreed to put on a show at Daw Aung San Suu Kyi's compound in Rangoon, at a two-thousand-strong party to mark the forty-eighth anniversary of Burma's independence from Britain. The comedians discussed the dangers of the invitation carefully before going, and decided that one brother at least should stay behind so that he might provide for the family and keep the troupe going if the others were arrested.

The show received rapturous applause from the party goers. Many of the jokes made fun of the direness of the country's leadership: in one routine, the troupe sang a satire about Burma's generals; in another, government workers were portrayed as thieves. On January 7 the troupe had returned home to Mandalay, but shortly afterwards many of their number were arrested by officers from Military Intelligence Unit 16. Eight were released a month later, but U Pa Pa Lay and U Lu Zaw were charged under Section 5e of the 1950 Emergency Provisions Act with spreading "false news, knowing beforehand that it is untrue." The following March they were sentenced to the maximum seven-year prison term. Their trial was closed: when four NLD members—including Daw Aung San Suu Kyi herself—attempted to travel by train to Mandalay to appear as witnesses in the comedians' defense, they were informed that their railway car was "broken."

Since then news of the two men has been sketchy. At one point they were forced to work with iron bars shackled to their legs; then Pa Pa Lay was reported to be gravely ill. He was transferred from a labor camp to a prison, where he is now believed out of immediate danger. His wife visits the prison every other month; she is able to leave him a package of food, but is not permitted to see him. Lu Zaw remains in a remote labor camp.

Lu Ma, the brother who deliberately stayed behind, continues to run the troupe, but without official permission. Despite that, he often performs to groups of tourists. This he believes not only provides an income, but affords the troupe a measure of security. "I know I play with fire each day," he recently told the Norwegian newspaper *Aftenposten*. "I'm skating on thin ice. But I just want to be free to make my jokes."

Please write letters appealing for the release of U Pa Pa Lay and U Lu Zaw to:

Lieutenant General Khin Nyunt
Secretary 1
State Peace and Development Council
c/o Director of Defense Services Intelligence
Ministry of Defense
Signal Pagoda Road
Dagon Post Office
Yangon
Union of Myanmar
Fax: 011 951 222 950

Randolph Thomas

*I was five or six when this picture was taken,
and the event I am introducing, the reason for
the welcome sign, remains a mystery.*

Randolph Thomas earned an MFA in poetry writing from the University of Arkansas. His short stories have appeared in a number of magazines, including the *Hudson Review* and *Press*. His poems have appeared in *Poetry*, *Poetry Northwest*, the *Literary Review*, *Quarterly West*, *Witness*, and *Louisiana Literature*. In 1997, he was awarded a grant for his poetry from the Arkansas Arts Council, and in 1998 he attended the Sewanee Writers' Conference with a Tennessee Williams Fellowship in fiction. A native of southwestern Virginia, he has taught at the University of Arkansas, New River Community College, and, most recently, at James Madison University in Harrisonburg, Virginia.

RANDOLPH THOMAS
The Fortune

unt Ruth's money had nothing to do with any of us. The money came from her husband, Uncle Will, from his construction business, which he had taken over from his father, a man who had traveled to Roanoke by wagon in the 1870s, and risen to wealth and influence through his skills at underbidding. It had been Aunt Ruth's luck that Uncle Will was injured by a falling brick and landed in the hospital, that Aunt Ruth was his nurse. The couple fell in love, and Uncle Will proposed to her.

I don't know how much of this story Cousin Estella ever knew. She's never had much desire to know about family history or about anything west or south of the Piedmont, which is the attitude of most of our family here in Richmond, as well as in northern Virginia.

But Cousin Estella must at least know that Ruth's parents, our grandparents, died before they were forty, during a scarlet-fever epidemic, and that all ten of their children were farmed out to nearby families who raised them to eighteen. More than seventy years ago, the two youngest—Aunt Ruth and her sister, Aunt Christine—trained as nurses and went to work in a hospital in Roanoke, two hundred miles southwest, in the Allegheny Mountains. Over the years and decades, they

Glimmer Train Stories, Issue 39, Summer 2001
©*2001 Randolph Thomas*

became known as the Roanoke contingent of our family, and most of us only knew them from the reunions Uncle Karl and Aunt Opal held every year on their anniversary.

Aunt Ruth outlived all of her siblings, and for decades, the only word of her came from Aunt Christine's only child, poor Cousin Hugh Snydow, the playboy bachelor of our family and the only Roanoke cousin.

A number of us, especially Cousin Estella, became concerned about Aunt Ruth three years ago, when Hugh came up to see me while I was in the hospital, fighting a bout of pneumonia which was brought on by my emphysema. Cousin Estella was in the room with me, along with her husband Mitch. When Hugh came in they were talking over top of me like I was part of the furniture.

Poor Hugh's face was puffed out, and he staggered. His hair and eyes were wild. Cousin Estella asked him several times if he was feeling all right, and he acted like he didn't hear her. He grinned at Mitch, who was standing underneath the TV with his arms crossed.

"I've had a mild stroke," Hugh said finally. Estella and Mitch watched him like he'd admitted having a contagious disease.

"It wasn't much," he said, his eyes roving the room. "I was sitting in a booth at Haley's, eating a piece of pie, and all of a sudden I wasn't moving right. The waitress said there was a trickle of drool on my chin. It wasn't much. I was in the hospital a little over a week, and since then I've been in therapy."

"You're able to drive?" Estella said.

"I drove here," Hugh said, grinning with one side of his mouth. "I stop and rest."

"How's Aunt Ruth?" Estella said.

"Stone deaf," Hugh answered, "same as ever."

"I already know she's deaf," Cousin Estella said. "I want to know how she is otherwise."

"Her health is good," Hugh said, nodding idiotically, "except for her memory, which is almost as bad as her hearing. I get by to see her every day, to make sure she doesn't need anything."

"How's the house?" Estella said. "Isn't it a terrible burden for you?"

"I have a girlfriend from the church who helps me," Hugh said. He winked at Mitch.

Estella kept at Hugh with questions about Aunt Ruth, but he was never more than vague. When he was ready to leave, he walked over to the bed and shook my arm.

"Good-bye, old friend," he said. "Get better soon."

"Why don't you spend the night with us?" Estella said.

Mitch patted Hugh on the shoulder.

"After supper we can drink a cold one," he said. "That's a drive I wouldn't want to make twice in one day."

Estella followed Hugh down to the elevators. She complained later because Hugh let the door close on her, interrupting her in mid-sentence, proving he was incapable. Every afternoon that week, she was in my hospital room, worrying and wondering aloud. She was convinced Hugh was in no condition to take care of Aunt Ruth, who was in God knows what kind of shape.

"What do you know about them?" I wanted to say. When I was seventeen, I wanted to get away from the world I'd grown up in. I wanted to work for the Norfolk and Western Railroad. I wanted to be an engineer, and, as a stepping stone, I took a job in one of the welding shops in the Roanoke yards. I was down there for three or four months, until the war and the draft board changed my plans forever, and during that time I lived with Aunt Ruth and Uncle Will. When I came back from work, my skin and clothes would be thick with soot. Before Aunt Ruth could offer me tea or sandwiches, I'd go straight to the basement. I'd run the hose through the basement window, and I'd clean myself off down there, I was so worried to be in any room of their house and be so filthy.

I lived with them a short time, a long time ago, but there is plenty I remember: the parlor overlooking their backyard and Aunt Ruth's flower garden. On Saturday nights, other men Uncle Will knew or worked with and their wives came for cards and drinks, occasionally a late supper and a little dancing, and I would sit in their sun parlor by myself and read, although Aunt Ruth would come looking for me and cajole me into the room with the older people. Some nights Aunt Christine would come and bring little Hugh. By this time, Christine's husband had died, and looking at it now, I suppose she might have come looking for a rich, eligible bachelor. Aunt Ruth would pick up Hugh and carry him into the garden, make over him and spoil him the whole time they were there. Both Ruth and Uncle Will always treated Hugh like he was their own child, and I know for a fact they helped Christine send Hugh to college, whatever good it did him.

In Cousin Estella's favor, the reason for her concern was as plain as the confused light behind Hugh's eyes. She began to call Hugh, asking him about Aunt Ruth, worrying him and frustrating herself by trying to decipher his vague answers. She even tried to call Aunt Ruth, but of course nobody ever answered there. I was worried about all of them, but I was in the hospital for two weeks total, and I was the weakest I've been since my POW days in Burma when my oldest boy finally wheeled me out. I stayed with his family for more than a week while I gathered my strength. His wife doesn't get along with Cousin Estella, so I heard little from her during that time, but almost as soon as I had begun to feel like myself again and had gone back home to worry over my vegetable garden and the sad state it had fallen into, she and Mitch barged into my kitchen, and she was dying to tell me about her latest confrontation with Hugh Snydow.

In her phone conversations with Hugh, she had demanded that she and Mitch be allowed to visit Aunt Ruth. Hugh came up with excuses: Either Ruth had a cold or a doctor's appointment, or Hugh was too busy to meet them. When Estella finally lost her temper and asked Hugh flat out what he was trying to hide, he told Estella that she was just a bored busybody since her own father had died. He told Estella she was sticking her nose where it didn't belong, that he saw no reason for them to come, and that she and Mitch were only after Ruth's money. Estella was so angry she hung up on Hugh.

"I have to see her for myself," Estella said. She was planning to go ahead with their trip without Hugh's permission. She wanted my blessing, and I told her it came with a price.

"Don't talk like a damn fool," Estella said. "You're not going on a five-hour car trip with us or anybody. Tell him, Mitch."

Mitch knew where to draw the line. He stared out the glass door at my garden, a beer in his hand, pretending not to hear her.

Estella raised her hands toward the ceiling and spoke my dead wife's name, said that she was only doing what she promised, looking after me as best she could, only I didn't want to cooperate.

"You miss the point," I said. "I know Aunt Ruth, or I knew her once, and I know Hugh better than you do. Whatever happens will go more smoothly if I'm along."

Both of them could see how badly I wanted to go, and the truth is I felt like my life depended on my going. I was in the middle of a debate with my children over my ability to live by myself. This trip, the idea of it, meant so much to me, proof of my own independence as much as an answer to my concerns over my aunt's well-being. The minute Estella mentioned going, I would have done anything to come along.

We left at six one Saturday morning. It had been nearly a decade since I'd been west on 460, and I was surprised at how little had changed along the four-lane into the hills and then mountains. Once we got in Roanoke, though, I was lost, surprised and envious that Mitch seemed to take the turns without thinking. Familiar sights like St. Elizabeth's and the H&C sign struck me as terribly out of place among the modern buildings of the skyline. I was anxious, antsy as I had been the first time I was away from home, and I wished we could have taken the time to see more of the downtown, especially along Campbell and Norfolk Avenues where the bridgeworks had been, but Mitch and Estella were in no mood for stopping or even slowing down.

Like everything else I recognized, Ruth's Victorian house came up on me suddenly, as we turned a typical corner. The sad disrepair of the house—the chipped and dirty paint, the overgrown yard—were more painful because the other houses in the neighborhood were so well kept.

Mitch parked at the curb. I climbed up from the backseat, braced myself with the roof, stepped onto the curb, and followed them up the sidewalk. Estella was already pointing out how part of the drain hung loose from the side of the house, how one of the upstairs windows was broken.

The TV was turned up so loud I could hear it through the door. Nobody answered when Mitch rang the bell and then beat on the door, and for the first time, I was more afraid than worried. We walked around the house, Mitch stretching to look in the few windows with curtains drawn back.

"What is it? What do you see?" Estella kept saying.

"All dark inside," Mitch answered. The backyard where Ruth's beautiful rock garden had been was so overgrown I had to work to keep to the path, and only once did I smile, when I saw Uncle Will's iron Scottish terrier, a lawn ornament that had once stood beside a goldfish pond long filled in.

Mitch reached the broken second-story window with a ladder we found in the garage. The house smelled of moth balls and antiseptic, although filth and dust were everywhere, so much dust as to make you sneeze. Ruth was living in her dining room; her bed was down there, in front of the blaring TV. All around the bed were empty ice-cream containers. Ice cream seemed to have made up the largest portion of her diet under Hugh's care.

"Hugh?" Ruth said. Her hair was thin and long, her mouth a cheery oval with two teeth jutting up from the bottom row.

"It's not Hugh," I said. I told her my name, which, like my face, meant nothing to her. The room had the odor of defecation, and Estella put her hand to her mouth to keep from gagging as she rushed to the bedside. "It's Estella," she said. "I'm your niece, Estella. You must remember."

"Hugh?" Aunt Ruth said again. There was rust on her face from lack of bathing.

In all the rooms, wallpaper hung down in long strips or swelled out from the wall or the ceiling. In the living room, furniture slipcovers were torn and stuffing stuck out in places. I looked into the glass cases of trinkets, the collectibles from her travels with Uncle Will: to Europe in the twenties, to Panama when the canal was being built, to Havana where the couple gambled in the late forties. Many of the cases stood open, their contents shuffled and overturned, and I had a disturbing image in mind of Hugh exploring the house while she slept or called out his name, opening the cases and playing with the tiny porcelain Bavarians, the clay bears and tea settings, a child in her house again.

The parlor where I read and listened to the voices and laughter from their social events was curtained off, cold and bare except for a few dead plants placed on a little table, probably for sunlight, and then forgotten. The drawers of the table were pulled out and turned upside-down on the concrete floor. The contents—old letters, loose and in bundles—lay about the floor. I bent over and picked up a bundle. As soon as I lifted it, the rubber band snapped and letters scattered.

I could hear Estella and Mitch fussing over Ruth in the other room as she moaned and called out for Hugh.

"I think you ought to call him," Mitch said.

"I ought to kill him," Estella said.

Some of the letters were a hundred years old. Some were written by Uncle Will's father, the pages covered in the meticulous script of a man who had struggled to educate himself. Others had been written to him, some from men and women whose names I recognized or at least thought I had heard before: relatives and friends, Roanoke mayors and councilmen, state legislators. I was thinking that the letters needed to be gone through, that some of them probably ought to be in a museum or library.

Estella called me, and I put the letters down on the table between two dead plants. I went into the living room. Mitch was looking out the front window and scratching his head. Estella was holding the phone, dialing.

"The parlor," I said. "There's a table in there full of letters."

"We can worry about that later," Estella said. Hugh picked up right then, and she told him where we were and how unhappy we were with what we'd found.

"Ice cream's all she can get down," Hugh explained. "Her throat swells shut and she can't swallow anything else."

"It's not just the ice cream," Estella said, "if that wasn't bad enough." She informed Hugh she was bringing Ruth back to Richmond, that she was going to get a lawyer, prove he was *non compos mentis* if she had to.

"Let me speak to him," I said, but by the time I'd wrenched the phone from Estella's hands, there was just dial tone.

Estella said Hugh didn't matter, that, in fact, it was better to keep Hugh as far away as possible. Mitch took his camera out of the trunk of their car and made pictures of the house, inside and out, and of Aunt Ruth and the room she'd been living in. We wrapped a blanket around Aunt Ruth's shoulders and the two of them helped her out to the car. She rode in the backseat with me, and I watched her sleep on the long drive back to Richmond, much of it in the dark.

Over the next few days and weeks, I tried to call Hugh, but he wasn't answering the phone, wouldn't return the messages I left. Like she promised, Estella took Ruth's power of attorney away from him, and he didn't put up any fight. Like a haze closing over the mountains, this was the beginning of the final split with the Roanoke contingent, which now amounted to Cousin Hugh Snydow alone.

Estella celebrated her victory by cleaning Aunt Ruth up, buying her new clothes, and holding an open house. Cousins and their families from Richmond and northern Virginia filed through and spoke to Aunt Ruth, but she didn't know any of us. Estella hired a nurse to come several times a week, but Ruth needed constant supervision; after looking at the costs of live-in nurses and nursing homes, Estella and Mitch eventually settled on the home. Estella insisted that Ruth's trust was a very small fortune but certainly enough to cover her stay at a health-care facility.

A couple of times I rode out there with Estella and Mitch, visited Aunt Ruth and saw no change, except in her weight loss. Estella insisted that things would have been different if Ruth had known what was happening to her, but she didn't, and she was as happy in the home as she would have been anyplace else, except maybe in Roanoke with Hugh Snydow shoveling ice cream down her throat, and everyone agreed she would have died a lot sooner there.

Two and a half years after we took Aunt Ruth, I called Hugh to tell him she was dead.

"Dead," he repeated, like it was the first time he'd ever heard of anybody being dead. I told him Ruth hadn't been in any pain, that she had taken an afternoon nap and not woken up from it. I asked Hugh how he was doing; I wanted to talk longer, but he had every reason to distrust me. He said he had to get off the phone, that he was late for a church social.

I called him back several times with important information

as I learned it. Each time I got his machine, his slow voice that had never improved since his stroke, asking the caller to leave a message, which I did: the name of the funeral home, dates and times of visiting hours and services, the time and location of the burial.

All the minister knew about Ruth was her denomination, about as much as most in attendance knew. I looked for Hugh at the funeral home, and by the time we drove out to the gravesite, I'd pretty much given up all hope that he'd come. The day was sunny and warm. By this time, I'd lost my battle to live by myself, and I was living with my eldest son, whom I had on my right, my daughter-in-law on my left, holding onto me like I might drop any minute.

Fifty or more people, not counting kids. I was standing right up front, and I'll have to admit I was lost in my own thoughts. I didn't know the minister had stopped preaching until I felt a hand touch my shoulder. I came to my senses and realized that Mitch had moved over beside me.

"Take a look back yonder," he said. I turned to see what he meant, why everyone else was turning, cupping their hands above their eyes to see.

The sun was behind the car at the curb—a tiny, banged-up Japanese car, turquoise blue.

Hugh was at the driver's window, his puffy face all but filling it, his eyes red with tears.

"Why doesn't he come down and join us?" Mitch said. "Let bygones go by."

"Nothing doing," I said. "He'll not set foot from that car. I'll bet you any amount."

Estella marched to the curb, to the car, which rocked back and forth as Hugh played footsy with the gas and the clutch. Hugh rolled down his window.

"You monster," he began, "you monstrous bitch." Mitch

shook and started forward, but I grabbed hold of his arm so tightly he would have had to push me down to make me let go.

Hugh cussed Estella for sticking her nose where it didn't belong, for stealing his aunt.

"I only did what was best," Estella cried.

"What was best for you," Hugh said. He rolled up his window, having said his truth, which must have been about all he had left. The car jolted into gear and rolled away, leaving Estella to dab her eyes with a tissue before she returned to us.

When we got back to Estella's, the gathering was a lot like the reunions Uncle Karl and Aunt Opal used to throw. Estella had a big enough spread to feed two families besides ours. Buttercups were popping up in the little rock garden beside her drive and the children ran about the yard and played while all of us sat on the deck and ate off paper plates and drank coffee in styrofoam cups.

There were old times in our talk, reminiscences, tales of family past. Folks who had never before heard of Cousin Hugh Snydow chattered about how crazy he looked. They said it was hard to believe a man in that kind of shape had driven all that way in that tiny car just so he could cuss Estella, then drive all the way back.

Nobody wanted to leave. All afternoon there were people looking at their watches and saying, "I've got to be getting on," long, long before any of them did, and now it was starting to get dark. People were sleepy from all that good food, and some of the play on the lawn turned rowdy—as it always does when kids get together for long enough—with pushing and shoving and wrestling. Some parents had to be called on to pull some of the kids apart and separate them.

Estella told me she had something for me, a present she had saved before Aunt Ruth's furniture and antiques had been auctioned, all the money rolled over into her trust. Estella acted like it was something I had been interested in.

My present was the little table from Aunt Ruth's parlor, the one that had been covered with dust and filth, plus three or four dead potted plants. The table had been cleaned and polished. I opened all the drawers, and of course, the letters were gone, probably thrown away. Mitch carried the little table out to my son's station wagon, and I tried to look pleased when I thanked Estella.

I took out my handkerchief and dabbed sweat from my face, sat down on the steps of Estella's porch while I caught my breath. The table had started me thinking about Aunt Ruth's parlor, how I would sit in there on summer nights, reading books I have long since forgotten, listening to the voices of the older people, probably only in their late thirties, drinking and playing cards in the other room.

Estella was in the yard, saying good-bye to my grand-daughter and her husband. She leaned forward to make goo-goo talk to their baby.

"It's been so good to see everybody," I said, still day-dreaming. Nobody was close enough to hear me, and my voice sounded like paper crinkling. Across the yard, Estella lifted my most precious baby, my great-grandson, from his mother's arms. She held him up to admire and love.

Rita D. Costello

*Me, before tattoos, at an air show in Niagara Falls.
My friend Miche says she'd pay me to wear
a hat like this again: "...I'll buy the hat!"*

Rita D. Costello teaches composition, literature, and creative writing at the University of Louisiana at Lafayette where she is working on her PhD. She received her BFA in creative writing from Bowling Green State University in Ohio and her MFA from Wichita State University in Kansas. She has published poetry, short stories, and artwork in numerous journals, including *Fireweed*, *Illuminations*, the *Baltimore Review*, *Seattle Review*, and *the Slate*.

RITA D. COSTELLO
shadow trees

What a surprise it must have been   to learn
that a shadow has substance, to learn   that the absence
of light can last forever, both   in the place where it exists
and elsewhere. All the trees of Hiroshima had long
burned away before   I learned of their enigmatic
permanence; their dark-etched limbs, frozen   intimations
of growth which cannot enact their purpose, even

defy it. My mother would have killed me   if
she ever found me there, with my leg   propped up beneath the needle.
Jennifer's right hand smoothed out the skin   and held it taut
between two fingers, while the other held the needle, a finely pointed
sewing needle, wrapped tight   with a coil of thread, dipped first
in a bottle-cap filled with india ink   and then rapidly
piercing into my ankle the shadow   of my first tree

at fifteen. I went back to New York; the old elementary school   where
I once knelt in the cold hallways, with the crown of my head
pressed tight   into the circle formed by wall, floor, knees.
Every random drill, for six years, meant   another sleepless night
for my mother, desperate   to explain how unlikely a bomb could be. But
she never said, *there have been so few*; although dates and times
might have calmed me, a history lesson of that sort   advocates shadows

RITA D. COSTELLO

rather than enlightenment. I imagined at once   that the shadows
should have burned white: a testament   to lack and empty space,
but they didn't. Instead   dark stains traced trees and people
into the landscape, instantly   what was lost was perceived again
as presence. And we have to claim our shadows

as illumination. Silhouetted trees bloomed randomly
across my body in college, my wrist, shoulders, neck, back;
black ink only, limbs   without definition or leaves. It was
such a surprise to discover the power of shadows   that I couldn't
stop pressing them into my skin.

POETRY OPEN
1st-, 2nd-, and 3rd-Place Winners

First-place winner: RITA D. COSTELLO
"shadow trees"
Rita D. Costello receives $500 for her first-place poem, which begins on page 137, preceded by her profile on page 136.

Second-place winner: MARJORIE KOWALSKI COLE
"A Heart That Is Pleased by the Sea"
Marjorie Kowalski Cole, a resident of Alaska for thirty-five years, has published fiction and poetry in numerous journals including Chattahoochee Review, Cream City Review, Passages North, Room of One's Own, *and* Alaska Quarterly Review. *Her work has won several awards, and she has also written for* Poets and Writers Magazine *and* National Catholic Reporter. *She worked as a librarian for fifteen years and now writes full time, teaches occasionally, and enjoys the company of her two sons.*

Third-place winner: CLARK KAROSES
"a singed pigeon's quill"
Clark Karoses was born in Sheboygan, Wisconsin, and has lived most of his life in the Northwest. He is currently in the process of completing his MFA in creative writing at the University of Idaho in Moscow while raising his beautiful, one-and-a-half-year-old daughter.

We invite you to our website (www.glimmertrain.com) to see a listing of the top twenty-five winners and finalists, and online submission procedures. We thank all entrants for sending in their work.

Mark Rader

*I'm five and have apparently just discovered
scissors. I'd be a pretty intimidating pirate
if it weren't for the Forrest Gump shirt.*

Mark Rader is twenty-four years old and this is his first published story, not counting the publication of "I, Little Runner, the Hero," the story of a one-armed cave boy who saves his clan from a bear, which appeared in a kids' magazine in the eighties. He grew up near Green Bay, Wisconsin, and received his bachelor's degree from Tulane University in New Orleans. He's currently a graduate student in creative writing at Cornell University in Ithaca, New York.

MARK RADER
The Round

*I*t happens with no warning whatsoever, in plain view of the four hundred seventeen people attending the concert: Josef Pansky, the withered old violinist, is struck by a heart attack and dies, dramatically, onstage, in his tuxedo. No one is more surprised than Josef, who had been immersed in a lovely memory moments before the attack. He had just put his violin on his knee and was beginning to relax. The next minute and a half would involve only the woodwinds, a call and response between the oboes and the flutes, so he took the liberty of looking out into the audience. It was a good crowd despite the weather. It had been snowing profusely on the drive over, and the roads were slippery. *I'm glad they came*, he thought. His eyes scanned for someone he knew, but they all seemed to be strangers—people young enough to be his children and grandchildren. He was turning back to his music when, out of the corner of his eye, Josef caught sight of a woman wearing a blue dress with a spangle of peach-colored tulips embroidered across the front, which was—*could it be?*— the same dress his mother wore one summer when he was a boy. In the few years since turning eighty Josef was finding that memories of his childhood, filed away for years, were returning to him, vividly, a rare gift of advanced age, and here

Glimmer Train Stories, Issue 39, Summer 2001
©*2001 Mark Rader*

was another. From this fleeting image, he recreated his mother, forty years dead, rocking on the porch swing of their rented house that long-ago summer, her dress flapping in the wind, and then Josef wondered: Was that the place with the gnarly oak tree out front; and had that been the summer the Jaworskis' golden retriever had leapt at his face and knocked out his first loose tooth; and whatever happened to Ollie and Miroslav, the tow-headed neighbor boys he used to race through the sea grass? And, so engrossed in this recaptured memory was Josef, that he completely missed his entrance.

Josef's heart zipped high into his ribcage as he clumsily threw his violin onto his shoulder, and, for the first cloudy moments, as bows churned steadily around him, he puzzled at the stark alien shapes—ovals, dots, and lines—assembled on the page in front of him. He located his bearings and his place in the music, jumping in after a half rest, but felt his ears and neck glowing warm with embarrassment. Then it hit—a spike of heat shooting through his bowing arm that stunned his heart. He didn't have time to think. His body suddenly became heavy, the little strength he had left at eighty-three gushing out of him as if from a burst tire. Amazingly, within the minute, he was dead.

Three rows from the front of the stage a handsome thirty-eight-year-old chiropractor named Charlie has been sitting comfortably in his seat, curling the night's program in his hands. He is on a date with a blue-eyed twenty-five year old named Olivia, whom he met at the gym. He noticed her on the fly-weight machine, and was instantly taken by the way she worked out. She went about her business in the most exquisitely methodical fashion, and her posture was impeccable. It made her appear regal, even in spandex. Charlie introduced himself in line at the smoothie bar, made small talk about the weather, the crowds in the gym at lunchtime, asked her what she did (marketing), where she was from (Tallahassee), how long she'd been in town (five months). He flashed his winning smile as often as possible, hung on her every word, and then scribbled his home number on one of his ivory embossed business cards, and said, very casually, that he would love to take her out sometime. He could tell she liked his boldness and expected her to call back within the week, and, three days later, she did.

A night at the symphony is not something Charlie particularly enjoys, but he's taken Olivia here because women seem to appreciate the experience, especially the young ones who are used to nightclubs and men in silk shirts. It makes them feel tasteful. Charlie can tell it's working again. Olivia's head is tilted to one side, her arms loosely crossed, her back primly pressed against the back of the seat, and when Charlie turns to catch her eye, she smiles: not just a smile of acknowledgment, but a smile, he thinks, that bodes well for later.

There are those who belittle his lifestyle, who, out of jealousy, have called him, to his face and behind his back, pathetic and misguided. You're too old for this, they tell him. Charlie pictures them and smirks: his brother, poor, crew-cutted, potbellied Jerry, now with three chubby kids, lying on his sofa watching some awful TV movie with a discount beer in his hand; James, his sad, divorced, religious colleague kneeling at the foot of his bed in his pajamas, his hands clasped and his face mournful; and Shelly, the overweight office receptionist, out at a singles bar with her girlfriends, staring wistfully at the men she'll never have. If they only knew the feeling! he thinks. The absolute rush of freedom! The thrill of being totally alive! Here he is, a man of thirty-eight: his body is flush from a workout three hours ago; his hair, a conservative cut that allows a single rebellious lock to curl down near his right eyebrow, is in its peak condition, full and golden; and just the right amount of cologne lingers near his chest. And while the rest of the world is huddling inside their mortgaged houses waiting for something good to happen to them, *he* is out in the world on a bitter cold night with a beautiful woman.

It is now the middle of the adagio movement. The strings put down their instruments, the woodwinds begin a section by themselves, and Charlie settles his eyes on the old man in the second-violin section. The old man is looking out into the crowd, his eyes blinking, large and liquid, behind his thick black glasses. Before the performance started, Charlie watched the old man shuffle in, turkey-like wattles under his chin, grabbing on to music stands for support as he made a wobbly path to his chair. Charlie smiled to himself and found the man's small biography in the program. His credentials were surprising. Concertmaster of the Cincinnati Symphony Orchestra, 1946–1975. Educated at Juilliard. Soloist with orchestras on five continents. It is amazing, and Charlie knows he should feel inspired by the man's persistence, but he can't. Old people make him uncomfortable, with their awful helplessness, their desperate, hopeful hanging-on.

When the old man misses his entrance Charlie can't help but cringe. He turns to Olivia to see if she's noticed, but she is looking at the bass players. Then, suddenly, he hears the sound of wood hitting wood. Turning back to the stage, Charlie realizes the old man's violin has fallen out of his hand. His head then slumps against his chest, and his bow falls out of his right hand and snaps to the floor. He tips over slowly, the shifting weight of his body making the chair grunt against the floor, and lands, a sack of flour with legs, on his left side. It happens just like that, in steps, as if he is performing some macabre military maneuver. The orchestra stops haphazardly. Aborted notes linger in the air.

In seconds the concertmistress, a redheaded woman, is kneeling next to the old man. She shakes him a few times, then turns her face to the audience, and Charlie sees that she isn't nearly as attractive as he had imagined from her profile. Her eyes are closer together than he'd thought, rather rat-like, and her eyebrows are plucked into sinister arches. She shouts in a tone bordering on the maniacal: "We need a doctor! Is anybody here a doctor?"

Yes, a doctor, Charlie thinks, snapping out of it. Jesus Christ, someone help this man! Time, surely, is running out. The man could still be alive! Then he feels his shoulder moving and realizes Olivia is shaking him. Her face is fearful, her mouth open to reveal a neat set of teeth. "Charlie, for God's sakes, do something!" she says. Instantly, other faces swivel towards him, fear and urgency in their eyes. Olivia's logic dawns on him, horribly. For Chrissakes, he's a chiropractor! A chiropractor! But he sees how pointless it would be to argue. "Okay," he says, too loudly, and bolts out of his seat. He scissors his way past the held-in knees in the row, takes four long strides down the carpeted aisle, and leaps, impressively for a man of thirty-eight, onto the brightly lit stage.

Josef wouldn't have said he was obsessed with dying in recent years. He would have said that he was simply more aware of it than he used to be, just as he had become more aware of his lack of regularity and the obituary page. Dying was inevitable, the universal leveling stick, but what could you do about it? Many friends and relatives of his had spent their last years taking inventory on the sum of their lives. They cursed missed opportunities, assigned blame for their failures to the most unlikely candidates. But not Josef. He was satisfied with his life. He had been more successful than he'd ever imagined possible. Though his years had been riddled with pain and disappointment and bad behavior—he'd never had children, which he had started regretting only since his career had tapered off; he'd cheated on his first wife frequently; he'd been unnecessarily cruel to young musicians he considered a threat—despite all this, he told himself he would live his life the same way if he had the chance to do it over again. He had had great friends, traveled the world, dearly loved his two wives, now both dead and gone, and he had earned a living performing the music he loved. He had been lucky.

The way Josef worried about death was to worry about what came after. He had considered the scenario he read about in New Age books given to him by his niece—that when you die you enter a bath of light, and a communion of old friends and relatives in white robes call your name and surround you with radiant love. To boot, you get all the things you ever wanted and you are never sad. He had considered what his cellist friend Wayne Ko believed—that you would come back in a different form, as a caterpillar, a tree, an antelope, another person if you're lucky, and he had cringed at the possibility of munching on leaves for a lifetime. He had considered what his mother, a devout Roman Catholic, had told him after he had committed some childhood crime or another—that if he lived a life of sin, he would land butt-first on the Devil's pitchfork. But Hell seemed an antiquated notion to him in his old age, an old wives' tale passed down by generations of mothers hoping to discipline their children. And, of course, he couldn't help consider that there was absolutely nothing after dying. No heaven, no hell, no perception, nothing. Of all the possibilities he had considered, this had seemed to him the most horrifying, and the most probable.

So, considering all the years of conjecture, what is the feeling that comes to Josef when he finds himself, or what remains of himself, floating high in the rafters of the auditorium above the same crowd he had been playing for moments earlier? Relief, boundless relief, and surprise.

In this new form Josef realizes he has no eyes, no mouth, no ears—to be expected, really—yet he can see everything: above him the sooty-faced cherubs carved into the ceiling; below him, tops of heads and the tiled tan floor; and when he thinks, *Hello,* it is sounded in a voice that was his as a young man, free of the creaks and tremors he has been recently accustomed to, and he can hear this voice clearly. He finds that he can also move about with a freedom that is frightening. He can swoop down right next to someone, in an instant. All he has to do is think it, and, *bing!,* there he is.

His new powers are astonishing, but something seems off. It is uncomfortably quiet. He has nearly forgotten why in his excitement. He looks to the stage. There is a horseshoe of people around his lifeless body. A well-dressed man, his tie flung over his shoulder, his shirtsleeves rolled up to his elbows, is pounding his palm flat against Josef's body's chest. Josef thinks: *There,* and he is. The body looks familiar, like a painting one walks past everyday is familiar, but Josef does not feel he possesses it. It is rather comical, actually, this rubbery puppet with its ghostly pale ears long and stretched and wrinkled like dried fruit, its mouth open as if caught in mid-gasp.

There is a general rustling and murmuring coming from the crowd, erratic and underwater-sounding. The well-dressed man breathes loudly as he labors over Josef's dead body. Everyone seems to be waiting—waiting for what? Josef yells into the man's ear, but the man cannot hear him. *Give it up! It's no use! I'm dead!* He's said it hundreds of times, in jest, and here, finally, it's true. A thin man, a flutist, Josef believes, says he will call an ambulance and sprints off. Soon enough the man stops pumping. Someone suggests carrying the body off the stage, and four men—two cellists and two clarinetists—grab the body, tenderly, by the armpits and the ankles, and do so.

The conductor, a young man named Alfred Rosenstein,

fresh out of the conservatory, is totally overcome, Josef can tell. In fact, it's more than a guess—Josef can feel what the man is feeling, intensely, as if he is curled up in Alfred's ribcage. It is an awesome sensation, this immersion in another. Alfred does not know if they should continue. Alfred fears people see him as a petulant taskmaster already, and continuing with the concert in these circumstances would only cement his reputation as a heartless tyrant. He thinks, what would Bernstein do? Josef hovers near the conductor. *Play!* he yells. *People will understand!*

Alfred decides to consult with the executive director of the symphony, who is standing backstage. It's your call, says the executive director, a sandy-haired, somber man in a grey suit. The executive director nervously pulls at his left eyebrow until Alfred says he thinks they should stop the concert.

Alfred solemnly steps back to the podium and tells the audience he does not know what to say really, that this is just a terrible loss, and that he is very sorry, but he feels, under the circumstances, that the concert should be postponed. The crowd, thankful for some kind of cue, begins to talk at a normal volume.

Josef can't remember ever feeling such a profound sense of disappointment. It feels as if some principle, some truth, has been violated. What makes the moment worse is that he can feel disappointment elsewhere, strings of it traveling to him, like the tremors a spider must feel vibrating along a web under its feet. There in Row D, Seat 34: a woman wearing her best evening dress thinking, *Just my fucking luck.* She had made a special effort to get her children a sitter, so she could listen to this music performed live, music that she listens to on her headphones to calm herself while she vacuums, irons, and then exercises on her Nordic Track. And three seats down: an elderly couple who have had season tickets for over forty years, now dreading the rest of the evening, the awkward drive home in bad weather, a shared death sitting like an unwelcome hitchhiker between them. And ten rows up: a young couple on their first date, uncomfortable in their ironed clothes, feeling as if this is a premonition of bad things to come. And, scattered throughout the orchestra, many hearts feeling the same thing, or variations of the same thing—that there would be no other concert, for this was the last of the season, that all their hours of practicing, of sacrificing to make this music had been in vain.

Keep playing! Keep playing, dammit! Josef shouts now, fanatically. *You don't need this idiot to play!* There is something malicious about the atmosphere now, something desperate. Very few people have left. Strangers are talking to each other. *Did you see it?... Dropped like a felled tree... I've never in my whole life seen someone die before... At least he died doing what he loved...* Josef feels like crying. Can he cry anymore? What good is it to have the best seat in the house, to be able to feel the hearts, the desires of those below, and not be able to share it with anyone? What good is it to have crystalline hearing with nothing to listen to? He shouts out once more, *Play!* and he adds, *Sing!* but against all these dead ears, it sounds unbearably foolish.

Up in the balcony sits a girl named Alison. She is five. She is the daughter of the tuba player, and this is where she insists on sitting during his concerts. She likes to be taller than everybody else for a change. She is scared, because she has seen everything happen, so she is humming to herself. This is what she does when she gets scared, she hums. She is scared, but also sad. She's sad because she knows the man who fell over. His name is Josef. Her father had invited him to their apartment one night to drink wine. She had been scared of him at first, because he talked funny, but her father told her that this

was because he was born in a different country. He had an
accent. At the end of the night Josef had taken out his violin
and played "Mary Had a Little Lamb." In return, she had sung
"I'm a Little Teapot" for him and acted it out, bending her
arm into a handle and leaning over to pour imaginary tea
onto the living-room carpet.

Alison wishes it weren't so quiet. She can see her father
down below, and she wishes he would look up at her, but he
is talking to a man sitting next to him and is shaking his head.
Still humming, she looks up to see the angels in the ceiling.
Then she lets out a gasp. It's Josef. She blinks twice, slowly.
Her father has told her to do this, when she thinks she sees a
monster in her room, and it usually works—the monster
turns out to be her stuffed dinosaur, Toby, or a dress hanging
in her closet. She hums louder, but he is still there, floating,
bluish and hazy, and dressed still in his tuxedo. Then she sees
Josef turn his ghostly head as if he's heard her thoughts, and
suddenly he is right beside her.

Though his image is made of something close to mist, she
can still detect a further liquidity in his eyes, a sheen of
happiness. She feels brave. *I heard you humming a song, could you
sing it for me?* he asks. No hello, how are you, just this question,
his eyes soft, deep, something to fall into. She looks around to
see if anyone else is seeing what she is seeing, but they don't
seem to notice. She asks if she should sing it out loud. He tells
her to sing as loud as she can. He says he will sing along with
her. She doesn't think twice. She stands up straight and takes a
big breath.

Charlie had actually believed he could save the man. He
was frightened, but, at the same time, oddly confident. He
had seen something like this on a television show, and when
he knelt down next to the old man it all came back to him. As
the stage lights shone down on him, bright and relentless,

Charlie pumped on the man's chest, gave him mouth-to-mouth, put his ear up to the man's cold lips, listening for any sign of life. He did this for five minutes, desperately, before someone put a hand on his shoulder. "You gave it your best shot," the person said. As Charlie stood and watched, four of

the orchestra members carried the old man offstage. "I'm sorry," he said, to no one in particular.

Now the body is gone and Charlie is sitting on one of the orchestra chairs, exhausted. He is bent over, his head in his hands, his elbows perched on his knees. Beads of sweat linger on his eyebrows before falling down onto his cheeks and his fingers. His shirt is soaked through. He thinks he should feel satisfied for having tried, but he doesn't. He closes his eyes and tries to slow down his breathing, but in the darkness is the old man's rubbery, cold face—its discolored blotches, its grotesque latticework of wrinkles, its dead, blank eyes. Charlie opens his eyes with a start and a shiver worms up his spine.

The house lights are still dimmed. People are leaning over their seats talking to their neighbors; their gestures are confused, their faces concerned. A man near the front exit picks up his coat gingerly, preparing to leave. Next to him a woman with large glasses is nervously biting her thumb. Then, at the edge of his vision, Charlie sees something fluttering, and when he turns and squints he sees it is Olivia. She is waving at him and smiling.

Charlie waves back and realizes he had actually forgotten she was there, watching him like everyone else in the crowd. She is smiling at him; her eyes seem kind. He notices how young her face looks, how trusting. He knows immediately he will be able to sleep with her after what has happened; he has been courageous and she will want to reward his courage. But when Charlie looks down at his feet and imagines himself naked with Olivia, and feels the thrust of sex in his joints, hears their breathing and moaning, smells their mingling musks, it isn't excitement or joy or lust he feels—it is dread and inexplicable sadness.

Then, out of the blue, this elfin lilting voice from the balcony. Singing. Everyone else turns, as Charlie does, to find the voice, to make out the words.

Row, row, row your boat, gently down the stream.
Merrily, merrily, merrily, merrily, life is but a dream…

The little girl sings it again and again, and apparently there is no one there to stop her, no parent, no well-meaning stranger to give her a polite shush. Where has she come from? And why is she singing? Charlie cannot, for the life of him, figure it out; and he's not the only one, based on the quizzical looks developing around him. For a second it seems like the girl is playing a joke, but what could the point of that be? It takes about three times through the song before Charlie begins to enjoy it, and ten before he remembers that his mother had sung this to him once as he made bubble castles in the bathtub. She would wiggle his little yellow boat around the castle, and for the *merrily, merrily, merrily* part, she would tickle his shoulders. It's true, this really did happen to him. How has he forgotten this? What else has he forgotten? Mercifully, the girl just keeps singing, and soon Charlie cannot help himself. In his head he sings along, in counterpart. When a cello player jumps in, playing out loud what he is singing inside, Charlie cannot help but grin like an idiot.

Josef has had many fine moments within the walls of a music hall. In Budapest, in 1953, after a performance of Kreisler's *Praeludium and Allegro* which surprised even him in its brilliance, the crowd clapped like mad for him, whistled; then, as a group, clapped in time, one, two, three, four, like fans at a soccer match, as he came onto the stage three times to take in their applause. In Madrid he'd once broken his A-string in the middle of Wieniawski's *Scherzo Tarantelle*, and continued on three strings, improvising his way through the rest. They roared *Bravo!* and one woman—he had never found out who—threw a lacy red brassiere at his feet.

But this, this:

Row, row, row your boat, gently down the stream.
Merrily, merrily, merrily, merrily, life is but a dream…

When the girl started with the song, it took Josef a second

to remember that it was a round, and he waited for her to sing it twice before jumping in. How pure, how unaffected her voice is, he thought. And now here he is improvising above and below the designated notes, singing thirds, hooking added grace notes. There is a tangible change in the mood of the room. One of the cellists has joined in. The cellist, Josef knows, started in as a joke, and planned on falling out after a few run-throughs, but then felt it would be cruel to the girl, who is singing so bravely. One of the flutists, then a few people from the audience start in, hearty souls doing it on a lark. It is gaining momentum, and each person in the round tries hard not to fall out of their part, to stay steady. A jolliness, a campfire feel warms the air. Normally people would be embarrassed at themselves, but they are justifying their exuberance because they are doing it for the little girl, and, yes, for Josef, that poor old man who had died before their eyes. The others who remain silent watch and listen, fully aware of the rarity of the moment, already thinking how they will explain what is happening to others.

Josef would like to believe this could go on forever, but he knows it will not. Time may not exist in the next realm, but here it still roars in two-four time. In three minutes and nine... eight... seven seconds it will stop. The tuba player will reluctantly feel the responsibility to stop this, and will make his way up to the balcony, put his hand on Alison's shoulder, and whisper, "That's enough, honey." Some people will clap, some will boo, and then they will start with the business of going home. Two days later, in the Talk of the Town column in the local paper, the little girl's performance will be mentioned. The columnist, a young man recently bumped up from writing obituaries, will compare the moment to something out of a fairy tale or a Cecil B. De Mille movie.

As Josef continues to sing, the future ribbons out in front of him. It so stuns him that he stops singing for a moment, before falling back in. He can see that the girl will grow up to be beautiful, pursued by many, and will marry a veterinarian who shares her love for horses. Josef knows the man who made a show of reviving his dead body will go home with his date, have sex with her, and then, later in the night, sitting on the edge of his tub, will cry softly into a towel. The woman who is now worrying about driving back home to her children and their babysitter will talk about picking up an instrument for almost four years before paying for her first piano lesson.

And though Josef wishes he could ignore it, there is tragedy radiating from this room also. A boy, the son of a man named Walter James, sitting now in Row G, Seat 27 will, in ten years, drown in a bathtub at a college fraternity party; Ellis Rose, the second trombonist now considering whether to jump in the round, will die of a brain aneurysm while on a twenty-fifth wedding-anniversary vacation with his wife Judith; and the great-granddaughter of the concertmistress will be raped and killed at gunpoint behind a pea-colored warehouse under the pale light of the moon. These scenes flash fiercest in Josef's vision, but there are more.

Josef can see his funeral just a few days away, the assembly—his many nieces and nephews, the young minister hired by the funeral home, some of the orchestra members, a few members of the audience who feel obligated to show their respects after witnessing his death. He can see the article in the paper with his dated glamour shot, the gravestone that already has the name and dates of his second wife, and the bright, almost fluorescent flowers scattered around it.

But, here, now, the round is still in glorious motion. What little they know of their lives, Josef thinks of all the people who will soon gather their coats, their programs, their instruments, and make their way home. They all will be surprised at how things turn out. How will it end? This is the question buried deep inside them all. How will it end? Ready at last to find out, Josef closes his new eyes and stops his new ears and lets himself go...

A light snow is falling when the crowd opens the doors. The little girl holds onto her father's free hand as they walk together towards their car, barely visible in the dim moonlight. Her feet work in double time to keep up. Her cheeks are already getting chilled by the air. Her mind is swirling with music.

The Last Pages

*Dorothy Grace Burmeister and
daughter Suzy Q, 1958*

GERARD VARNI

J often feel lost when I'm writing. But I don't mind; in fact, I like the emotions that being lost evokes—the unease and anxiety, the urge to explore, scrutinize, ascertain. I make plenty of mistakes, missteps along the way, but that's fine. I'm encouraged by James Joyce's contention that errors are merely portals to discovery. "Death's Noisy Herald" emerged from an article I read about artificial heart valves, and about how some patients complain that the devices can be distractingly loud. That thought led me to the poker-game scene. And things just got weirder from there. Here I am in front of the Racoon Lodge, lost in New York.

RITA D. COSTELLO

I grew up on an island in the Niagara River, which I think is why I've never quite gotten over the idea that something can be beautiful and destructive—undercutting its own existence—simultaneously. The literature that means the most to me disturbs me in some way. I like the idea of creating, disturbing, and undercutting space simultaneously. The bridging and cleaving of space is typically an issue in my poetry. Often I try to reconcile different times and/or historical periods without losing sight of contradictions even in the reconciliation. In this, my greatest fear is trivializing things that are too largely important. In the same vein, I have no fear of manipulating or revising my personal history for an aesthetic work, but is it fair to do the same with an historical detail or a scientific fact? These fears plague me whenever I write about any of my obsessions: Hiroshima and Nagasaki, the Holocaust, HUAC, the Human Genome Project, and so on.

MARK RADER

*W*hat I remember most vividly from my years of performing with the youth symphonies in my hometown isn't any particular performance, but instead the fear that would sweep over me as I stood behind the stage curtains, waiting for the house lights to dim. It happened every time: my palms would get red and sweaty, my polyester suit would start to feel extra itchy, and I'd start imagining how I might screw up. I could play a wrong note, forget to repeat a section, or miss an entrance: that would be pretty bad. But the absolute worst thing I could do would be something that brought the orchestra to a screeching halt, like breaking a string during a solo, fainting from the heat of the klieg lights, or accidently launching my bow into the brass section. For all my worrying, nothing traumatic ever did happen onstage. We'd play our set, pack up our instruments, and my parents would take me out for a post-concert frozen custard. In writing "The Round," I got to live through the kind of disastrous night at the symphony I'd always dreaded, without the personal embarrassment.

I first drafted "Redneck Boys" when I was teaching English in Thailand in 1992. I drafted it by pen and manual typewriter, wearing earplugs against the blast of the village P.A. systems. I couldn't finish the story then. But distance in space and culture gives me the kind of perspective I need to write with clarity about where I grew up. When I picked up the story again in 1999, the voice in the early draft told me how to finish.

It's risky to write about Appalachia. Even if you are Appalachian, you have to listen hard or you'll lapse into caricature. When I read grotesque or cute stories about the kind of people I grew up around, it's not that the details are unrecognizable to me. Some details are recognizable if I adjust my eyes and look at my place and its people from a certain perspective, and if I stop before I look too far. I've decided it's a matter of depth perception. And that's what I'd like my readers to take away from my fiction: depth perception for the culture I write about.

This photo was taken by my sister, Catherine, in a ruined orchard above the house where we grew up. Down below, you can see our hometown, Romney, West Virginia.

RANDOLPH THOMAS

*T*he Fortune" is yet another story I've rewritten many times over many years, beginning in the spring of 1995. This is a story I have given up, vowed I would never return to, a story I have placed at the bottom of my manuscript pile, or hidden away. But I have always returned to "The Fortune," and I am proud to have written about a power struggle in a southern family, where the stakes are redefined and the winners do not completely understand all that is lost when the torch is passed. But how do families survive together? How do we stand one another? Cousin Estella, my heroine, earns her right to the family's scepter through presumption and selfishness, through her unwillingness to assume dignity, through belligerence and courage, and surely her family will endure. For me, other fortunes of the story include the speaker's brief visit to Roanoke (one of my most beloved cities), and the creation of some of my favorite characters so far, especially Cousin Hugh Snydow, hero to the lost. I hope I will one day write about him again.

SERGIO GABRIEL WAISMAN

*T*o measure time (even before the invention of digital). To contain it in a hand-held device, to situate it in the wheels and gears of a man-made mechanism (or the combinations of zeros and ones in a chip smaller than a fingernail). In Cortázar's story "The Pursuer," Johnny, a jazz musician, notices the deceiving nature of time while riding the metro in Paris. He realizes that in the distance between any two stops he can fully experience an event that lasts much longer than the train ride itself. He can relive a childhood memory and every note of a fifteen-minute song ("Save It, Pretty Mama"), for example, in the span of one and a half minutes—all the while conscious of the fact that he is still on the metro, living both experiences simultaneously. This realization ultimately destroys him.

TIFFANY DREVER

I got the idea for the title of this story from a short trip I took on a rice barge down a minor river in Thailand. We drifted for two days on an uncomfortable, beat up, tin can of a boat, but saw so many wonderful details of ordinary life: wild groups of boys bathing, women doing laundry in pink plastic tubs, a group of saffron-robed monks, begging bowls in hand, setting off on a ferry.

It's the paraphernalia of everyday life that intrigues me: telling details like chipped toenail polish, or worn-out dog leashes, or stalwart mailboxes, that seem resonant of someone's life and which I try to include in my writing. Traveling wakes me up to these things, and so does living in New York, the world's biggest village.

Excerpts from

AARON COHEN

*T*his was one of the first books I ever wrote. I'm still trying to arrive at that original level of innocence.

Girls these days have COOTIES!

My sister, Patsy, tells my friends I eat spinach, and then they think I am wierd. YUCK! Yuck! I HATE SPINACH! I HATE PATSY!

Boy, do I hate my sister! She tattle tales and gets me in trouble. When I tell on her, I'm still the one that gets in trouble.

Patsy always wants to join in when I am playing with my friends. I don't understand that because I never play with her friends.

One day I was walking Patsy home from school when a big boy kept following us. I stopped to let him pass me, but he stopped also. I got really scared.

The boy pushed me against the wall and then I saw Patsy looking at me while she was laughing.

Then the big bully was about to call his friends when...

Patsy knocked the bully out!

Patsy said "Frankie, it's all in the 'wrist.' Stick with me, and you will be all right in life."

From that day on, they lived with a very, very happy life.

PAUL RAWLINS

𝒯hese are my parents, shown here without prior knowledge or consent in a picture that appears to have been taken by somebody tall. Their names are LaVere and LaJune, a coincidence that never struck me until I was in my twenties, and they have been married now for more than thirty-five years.

They taught their children—with varying degrees of success—to read, to work, to be honest and frugal; saw to it that we had music and swimming lessons, plenty of vegetables for dinner (not that we ate them), and some new clothes for school in the fall; attended scores of band concerts and wrestling meets and back-to-school nights. All the things that good parents do with little credit until a day when their children realize that they no longer fear growing up to be like Mom and Dad—they only hope to do so well.

166

PAST CONTRIBUTING AUTHORS AND ARTISTS
Many of issues 1 through 38 are available for eleven dollars each.

Robert A. Abel • Linsey Abrams • Steve Adams • Susan Alenick • Rosemary Altea • Julia Alvarez • A. Manette Ansay • Margaret Atwood • Kevin Bacon • Aida Baker • Russell Banks • Brad Barkley • Kyle Ann Bates • Richard Bausch • Robert Bausch • Charles Baxter • Ann Beattie • Barbara Bechtold • Cathie Beck • Jeff Becker • Janet Belding • Sallie Bingham • Kristen Birchett • Melanie Bishop • James Carlos Blake • Corinne Demas Bliss • Valerie Block • Joan Bohorfoush • Harold Brodkey • Danit Brown • Kurt McGinnis Brown • Paul Brownfield • Judy Budnitz • Christopher Bundy • Evan Burton • Michael Byers • Christine Byl • Gerard Byrne • Jack Cady • Annie Callan • Kevin Canty • Peter Carey • Ron Carlson • Brian Champeau • Mike Chasar • Robert Chibka • Carolyn Chute • George Makana Clark • Dennis Clemmens • Robert Cohen • Evan S. Connell • Ellen Cooney • Rand Richards Cooper • Wendy Counsil • William J. Cyr • Tristan Davies • Toi Derricotte • Janet Desaulniers • Tiziana di Marina • Junot Díaz • Stephen Dixon • Michael Dorris • Siobhan Dowd • Eugenie Doyle • Andre Dubus • Andre Dubus III • Wayne Dyer • Ron Egatz • Barbara Eiswerth • Mary Ellis • Susan Engberg • Lin Enger • James English • Tony Eprile • Louise Erdrich • Zoë Evamy • Nomi Eve • Edward Falco • Lisa Fetchko • Susan Fox • Michael Frank • Pete Fromm • Daniel Gabriel • Ernest Gaines • Tess Gallagher • Louis Gallo • Kent Gardien • Ellen Gilchrist • Mary Gordon • Peter Gordon • Elizabeth Graver • Andrew Sean Greer • Gail Greiner • John Griesemer • Paul Griner • Patricia Hampl • Christian Hansen • Elizabeth Logan Harris • Marina Harris • Erin Hart • Daniel Hayes • David Haynes • Daniel Hecht • Ursula Hegi • Amy Hempel • Andee Hochman • Alice Hoffman • Jack Holland • Noy Holland • Lucy Honig • Ann Hood • Linda Hornbuckle • David Huddle • Siri Hustvedt • Stewart David Ikeda • Lawson Fusao Inada • Elizabeth Inness-Brown • Bruce Jacobson • Andrea Jeyaveeran • Charles Johnson • Leslie Johnson • Wayne Johnson • Thom Jones • Tom Miller Juvik • Cyril Jones-Kellet • Elizabeth Judd • Jiri Kajanë • Hester Kaplan • Wayne Karlin • Andrea King Kelly • Thomas E. Kennedy • Jamaica Kincaid • Lily King • Maina wa Kinyatti • Carolyn Kizer • Carrie Knowles • David Koon • Karen Kovacik • Jake Kreilkamp • Marilyn Krysl • Frances Kuffel • Anatoly Kurchatkin • Victoria Lancelotta • Jennifer Levasseur • Doug Lawson • Don Lee • Peter Lefcourt • Jon Leon • Doris Lessing • Debra Levy • Janice Levy • Christine Liotta • Rosina Lippi-Green • David Long • Nathan Long • Salvatore Diego Lopez • Melissa Lowver • William Luvaas • Richard Lyons • Bruce Machart • Jeff MacNelly • R. Kevin Maler • George Manner • Jana Martin • Lee Martin • Alice Mattison • Jane McCafferty • Judith McClain • Cammie McGovern • Eileen McGuire • Susan McInnis • Gregory McNamee • Jenny Drake McPhee • Frank Michel • Nancy Middleton • Alyce Miller • Katherine Min • Mary McGarry Morris • Mary Morrissy • Bernard Mulligan • Abdelrahman Munif • Manuel Muñoz • Karen Munro • Kent Nelson • Sigrid Nunez • Ron Nyren • Joyce Carol Oates • Tim O'Brien • Vana O'Brien • Mary O'Dell • Chris Offutt • Laura Oliver • Felicia Olivera • Stewart O'Nan • Elizabeth Oness • Karen Outen • Mary Overton • Patricia Page • Peter Parsons • Roy Parvin • Karenmary Penn • Susan Perabo • Constance Pierce • Steven Polansky • John Prendergast • Jessica Printz • E. Annie Proulx • Kevin Rabalais • Jonathan Raban • George Rabasa • Margo Rabb • Paul Rawlins • Nancy Reisman • Linda Reynolds • Anne Rice • Alberto Ríos • Roxana Robinson • Paulette Roeske • Stan Rogal • Frank Ronan • Elizabeth Rosen • Janice Rosenberg • Jane Rosenzweig • Karen Sagstetter • Kiran Kaur Saini • Libby Schmais • Natalie Schoen • Jim Schumock • Lynn Sharon Schwartz • Barbara Scot • Amy Selwyn • Catherine Seto • Bob Shacochis • Evelyn Sharenov • Sally Shivnan • Ami Silber • Al Sim • George Singleton • Floyd Skloot • Roland Sodowsky • Gregory Spatz • Brent Spencer • L.M. Spencer • Lara Stapleton • Barbara Stevens • John Stinson • George Stolz • William Styron • Karen Swenson • Liz Szabla • Paul Theroux • Abigail Thomas • Randolph Thomas • Joyce Thompson • Patrick Tierney • Andrew Toos • Patricia Traxler • Jessica Treadway • Rob Trucks • Kathryn Trueblood • Carol Turner • Christine Turner • Kathleen Tyau • Michael Upchurch • Lee Upton • A. J. Verdelle • Daniel Villasenor • Daniel Wallace • Ren Wanding • Mary Yukari Waters • Jamie Weisman • Lance Weller • Ed Weyhing • Joan Wickersham • Lex Williford • Gary Wilson • Robin Winick • Terry Wolverton • Monica Wood • Christopher Woods • wormser • Celia Wren • Calvin Wright • Brennen Wysong • Jane Zwinger

Coming soon:

I start with an image, a resonant visual image that stays with me. And I have some sense of the feeling of the end of the story, where I want to end up. Then I discover what lies between this beginning and end.

from an interview with Vikram Chandra
by Jennifer Levasseur and Kevin Rabalais

When a few months had gone by and Zimmerman had still not taken a job he began to be called, as John had said, a *luftmensch*, a man who lives, so to speak, on air, without any visible means of support.

from "Inside the Wall" by Carl Schaffer

At first it appeared his wife, Jungmi, would never recover from her anger and shock, but along came a grandson, plump as a steamed pork bun; and then a black-eyed granddaughter with skin the color of richly steeped tea. They weren't the Korean babies Jungmi had wanted her daughters to have, but at least everyone was communicating again.

from "White Fate" by Carol Roh-Spaulding